REVENGE

THE SECOND CHAD HAMILTON NOVEL

MIKE SHANE

Cover design by Spiffing Covers

REVENGE

THE SECOND CHAD HAMILTON NOVEL

MIKE SHANE

"Revenge is always sweet. It's the aftertaste that is bitter."

Joshua Caleb

BOOK ONE

THE HOOK

CHAPTER ONE

"IF THIS IS HEAVEN, sign me up!"

Chad smiled, sitting on his deck chair, looking up into the pale blue sky with its white marshmallow clouds. "Me too Mac. It's the closest thing to paradise I've ever experienced. The first time I went sailing I was eleven. I didn't want to go back at the end of the day." Chad was pulling on the rope that was attached to the sails. He unconsciously touched his chest as he felt a twinge of pain.

"Careful sailor. It's only been five months," Mackenzie said.

"I know, I know, but the wind is so exhilarating that I sometimes forget. Right now I feel like the king of the world. Leonardo DiCaprio has nothing on me!"

"I sincerely hope not. Don't forget, the Titanic sank." Mackenzie did a three sixty as she scanned the horizon. "It is intimidating, isn't it? Not seeing anything but ocean all around. Makes you feel small in the whole scheme of things."

"I don't want to think at all. That's why we're out here all alone enjoying each other."

"Too late," Mackenzie said.

"What...why?"

"I see a boat."

"Where?"

Mackenzie pointed north, "Over there."

"Oh well. I suppose we can't expect to have the whole ocean to ourselves." Chad squinted through the bright sunlight, "I see it." He reached for the binoculars. "That's Alex Sanderson's boat."

"I don't believe it. Is there anyone you or Kade don't know?"

Chad grinned. "I didn't know you until six months ago when you needed rescuing."

Mackenzie jumped on Chad's lap, throwing her arms around his neck. "And I'll love you forever for it."

"Forever's a long time. How about another six months?" Mackenzie frowned. "Uh, what I meant was ten thousand years."

"I can live with that," she said. "As long as I have the right to renegotiate." She looked toward the other boat. "Shall we say hello to your friend?"

"He's not really a friend. I just see him and his wife and daughter once in a while on the dock. We do the usual chit chat. He likes to motor around for a few miles. Not the adventurous type. If he gets close, a honk and a wave will be sufficient."

Mackenzie took the binoculars. "Okay, I just wanted to be neighborly." Suddenly her countenance changed. "Chad, there's a little girl standing on the deck all alone."

"That's most likely the daughter I was telling you about. I'm sure everything is alright."

"Would you let our daughter stand on the deck all alone while we were down below doing who knows what?"

"I know exactly what we'd be doing," Chad teased. "So now we're married with a little girl? My my, Ms. Evans."

Mackenzie gave a small laugh but as the boat came closer, her concern deepened. "I have a bad feeling about this, Chad. It looks like she's crying."

Chad gently took the binoculars. "All I wanted was a nice quiet afternoon to spend with my lady." He looked up to the sky, shaking his head, and then looked through the binoculars. Even though the boat was still at least a mile away, Chad could see the girl's terrified face. There also seemed to be some kind of red substance on the front of her bright yellow bathing suit. "You're right Mac, something is wrong. We'd better take a look."

As they got closer and the binoculars were no longer needed, they both could see the girl was standing still, almost statuesque-like, crying uncontrollably.

As they got close to the boat, Chad yelled, "Ahoy on the boat! Alex, can you hear me? It's Chad Hamilton."

Nothing, only the sound of the little girl crying.

"Let's pull up beside it."

As they stopped next to the Sanderson boat, Chad helped Mackenzie up a rope ladder. As soon as she was standing firmly on the deck, the Sanderson's daughter ran towards her and jumped into her arms, gripping Mackenzie tightly around her neck.

Chad said, "Her name is Ellie. Stay with her while I check the cabin below."

Mackenzie nodded.

Working his way down the stairs, Chad had a hollow feeling in the pit of his stomach. He froze in his tracks when he reached the bottom and could see the entire cabin clearly. What he saw made him instantly sick. There was blood everywhere. Lying on the bed were the bodies of Alex and Janette Sanderson. Both had their hands tied behind their backs. It was painfully obvious they had been brutally stabbed and mutilated by some kind of sharp knife, maybe even a machete type weapon. Chad stood in shock and silence for a moment, and then knowing there was nothing he could do, slowly made his way back up the steps.

Mackenzie knew that whatever Chad had discovered, it was bad. "What's wrong?" she asked, not really wanting to know.

Chad stood motionless, then looked at her in disbelief. "We've got to call the Coast Guard. Whoever did this is long gone and they smashed their radio. Let's get her to our boat and I'll make the call."

As they made their way back to Chad's boat, little Ellie clung to Mackenzie and would not let go. She was silently sobbing and whispered, "I want my mommy."

"I know sweetheart. Let's get you on the boat first, then we are going to call someone to come and help your mommy and daddy. Would that be okay?"

If it was possible, Ellie clung even tighter to Mackenzie. Mackenzie sat on one of the deck chairs and began slowly rocking her.

Meanwhile, Chad radioed the Coast Guard, quickly explained the situation and gave their location. Then he took out his satellite phone and dialed a number he was all too familiar with. "Ender, this is Chad. I've got a bad situation here."

FBI Special Agent Andrew 'Ender' Brimhall asked, "What kind of trouble?"

Chad explained in detail the situation as best he could.

"Have you notified the Coast Guard?"

"Yes, they're on the way."

"Did you call Kade?"

"Not yet."

"Wow, I'm impressed. You are actually following proper procedure."

"Cut the sarcasm Ender. This is a bad one!"

"Sorry pal. You did the right thing. I can't do anything until the Coast Guard has taken charge and done their investigation. I'll be waiting for you at the harbor."

Chad hung up and speed dialed Kade. "What's up pal? I'm having lunch with a gorgeous detective at the moment which makes your call extremely inconvenient."

"We got trouble."

"Why does *we* always mean, *me*? I thought you and Mackenzie were out boating this morning? Don't tell me you ran over a whale or something?"

Chad said nothing.

"Uh oh, your silence tells me this is not good. What have you done?"

"In a nutshell, Mac and I were in fact sailing and came upon a boat with two bodies and a scared little girl covered in blood. She is their daughter."

"What can I do?"

Chad said, "At this point, I'm not sure. I was casually acquainted with these people. Their names were Alex and Janette Sanderson. They were brutally murdered, literally hacked to death by what I assume was some kind of machete. Whoever was responsible for this was definitely delivering a message. It reminds me of those campaigns we had in Africa when the warlords were terrorizing the locals." Chad paused for a moment. "See if Neal can research the Sandersons. Maybe he can use some of his magic and find something suspicious that might give us an insight as to what this is all about. You and I can meet up later. Mac has the little girl, Ellie, and she's not about to let go. She has latched on to her. I think the mom looked a lot like Mac, which maybe brings what little comfort there is for her. We're taking her to the hospital when we get ashore and someone from Child Welfare Services will meet us there. We are hoping they'll let us keep the girl temporarily. She's been through too much already. That'll give them and us a chance to locate relatives."

"How do you do it?"

"Do what?"

"Run into these messes?"

Chad sighed. "Just lucky I guess. All I wanted was a little time with Mackenzie. Is that asking too much?"

"I'll get back to you buddy."

———

AT THE HOSPITAL, the only way the nurses and doctors could check Ellie out was with Mackenzie holding her in her lap. She was still in total shock and since Chad and Mackenzie had found her crying on the boat, had barely uttered a sound. The doctor determined as best he could that Ellie was okay physically, but obviously needed to go see the in house psychiatrist for evaluation. While Mackenzie and the girl went up to the psychiatrist's office, Chad stayed in the lobby to talk with Agent Brimhall.

"What do you think Ender?"

"It's a little early yet, Chad, but the Coast Guard's preliminary investigation confirms pretty much what you feel, that it was an execution style homicide. Beyond that, they're not sure. Maybe the daughter will be able to tell us something. They've turned the case over to us at the FBI and I'll be the lead investigator." Ender smiled. "I'm assuming you've already got the Boy Wonder on it?"

"That I do." The Boy Wonder Ender was referring to was Neal, a computer whiz that met Chad almost a year earlier. He looked like the stereotypical geek, with long blond hair that never looked combed and two weeks overdue for a haircut. And at age 23, he was skinny as a rail. He was originally set up by Victor Steele, a ruthless billionaire corporate raider seeking revenge on Chad. After Steele's intentions were exposed and Steele was dealt with, Neal became Hamilton Industries' computer expert. There wasn't anything he couldn't do with a computer. When Agent Brimhall introduced him to two of the FBI's best computer analysts, Neal quickly made them believers in his genius. But he liked where he was. "I've got Neal digging into the Sandersons' backgrounds to see if he can find any dirt or indication as to why someone would want them eliminated. I'll let you know as soon as I know."

Mackenzie came walking up to Chad and Ender, Ellie holding tightly to her hand. She did not look happy.

"What's wrong?" Chad asked.

"Trouble!"

CHAPTER TWO

KADE COULDN'T BELIEVE Chad's luck. Discovering two bodies while out sailing was just sick. He wasn't completely recovered from their last escapade six months earlier when Chad was shot twice in the chest. He had only survived by some, almost unexplained, miracles. "Here we go again," mumbled Kade. He was on his way to an appointment after Chad called about the murder of the Sandersons. At least this was something that could be left alone and turned over to the authorities. *Right,* he thought. Under normal circumstances that would be the case. But therein lay the rub. There was nothing normal about Chad. No, not Chad Hamilton, savior of mankind; crusader to the downtrodden, and protector of the oppressed. Kade chuckled, "That's why I luv ya, big guy; never a dull moment." Kade calling Chad *big guy* was somewhat of an exaggeration. At 6'3" with massive shoulders that narrowed down to a slim waist, Kade was the big guy. But Chad was no slouch at 6'1" with an athletic build.

En route to a meeting with a distraught husband whose wife had left him, Kade had answered Chad's phone call. As owner of his own detective agency, Kade met with new clients regularly. As he pulled into the parking lot of the address he'd been given, he grabbed his cell phone and dialed a familiar phone number. "Good afternoon, young man."

"Hey, Kade," Neal said.

Kade said, "You aren't going to believe this, but Chad has run into a bit of trouble." Kade then rehearsed Chad and Mackenzie's morning on the ocean.

"Are you kidding me? How does he do it?"

"Who knows? Anyway, he wants you to do your magic and find out everything you can about the Sandersons. And of course, we need it yesterday."

"Okay, I'm on it."

Kade hung up the phone and got out of his car. "Okay, Mr. Wainwright, let's see what I can do for you." Arthur Wainwright was the client Kade was about to meet. As Kade got out of the elevator on the second floor of a nice business building, he immediately saw a smoked glass door that said Wainwright Enterprises. As he walked through the door, a smiling secretary met him. "I'll bet you're Mr. Kincaid."

"That I am, but please call me Kade."

"I'll call you anything you like, honey." She giggled.

Kade smiled politely. His surfer-like blond hair and pearl white teeth enhanced his wide smile. "Why, thank you. Aren't you sweet? Mr. Wainwright is here, I presume?"

"Yes, he's expecting you." She got up from her chair, walked to the door and knocked. "Arthur, Mr. Kincaid is here."

Wainwright got up from behind his desk and opened the door, extending his hand, "Mr. Kincaid, thank you for coming to see me," Wainwright was a pudgy 5'9" with pale, blotchy skin and dark greasy hair. Good grooming was not on his regular agenda.

"You're welcome. My friends call me Kade."

Wainwright pointed to a beige chair across from his desk, "Please sit down, Kade. Can I get you some coffee?"

"No thank you. So, Mr. Wainwright ..."

"Please, call me Art."

"Okay, Art, what kind of a business is this?"

"I'm in the import/export industry. I deal in just about everything, mostly small stuff. I act as a go-between. I'm more of a broker. It definitely keeps me hopping. I deal a lot with countries in Southeast Asia."

"Sounds interesting." Kade paused. "What is it that I can do for you, Art?"

Wainwright's countenance changed dramatically. "I'm afraid I've made some terrible decisions in regards to my wife. It's all my fault. I accept full responsibility for her leaving me."

"Why?"

"Well, I definitely got a lot of indicators. I've been so wrapped up in my work that over the last year or two I have totally neglected her. It's not like I didn't get sufficient warning. She has complained constantly and, I might add, not without justification."

"When did she disappear?"

"A few days ago."

"Do you have any idea where she might have gone?"

"No, I don't. I don't think it was very far. She doesn't have any family. We weren't able to have children so I'm all she's got. That's why I need to find her. She doesn't know it but she is still my whole life. I know if I can get her back I can convince her of that. I just need time to prove it to her. I've already booked a cruise for the two of us next month. I'm sorry to say it's the first decent thing I've done in, well, a long, long time. I've got to get her back. Please help me."

Kade said, "I'll do my best. Do you have a list of credit cards that she might have, or any other pertinent information such as favorite hotels, friends or anyone she might feel safe with?"

"Yes, I've made a list of anything that I think might help you. Please bring her back to me, Kade." Wainwright was a little teary-eyed.

"I'll find her, Art." *And then I'll find out just how sincere you are, Wainwright.*

———

"WHAT KIND OF TROUBLE?" Chad asked.

Mackenzie said, "The social worker, a Joan Calhoun, wants to take Ellie and put her in their custody and eventually into foster care, until a relative can be located."

"What if there is no relative?"

"That's what concerns me, Chad. This little girl has been through what is most likely the worst trauma a child could endure. She has obviously latched onto me. I think it needs to stay that way."

"What makes you think you're equipped for this?"

"I have no clue, but this isn't about me, it's about Ellie and her needs."

"I agree, but it still worries me. What about your workload and anything else going on in your life?"

"Like I said, it's not about me, it's about this poor little one." Ellie was still clinging tightly to Mackenzie.

Chad took a deep breath and let it out slowly. "Alright Mac. Where is Ms. Calhoun?"

"Right here, Mr. Hamilton," she said as she approached them with a stern look.

"Please call me Chad. Mackenzie and I want to help. What can we do?"

Joan Calhoun softened a bit. She looked mid-thirtyish with light brown hair pulled back neatly in a tight bun. Her skin was light and her dark eyes reflected a long day. "You two have been wonderful thus far. I think now it's time to let our organization take charge of Ellie's care. Unfortunately, we have a tremendous amount of experience with this type of situation."

Chad smiled. "Of that I have no doubt. I know for a fact that all of you at the Department of Child Welfare and Social Services are over-worked, underpaid, and under-appreciated. Look, Ms. Calhoun..."

"It's Joan."

"Okay, Joan, don't you think that it would be in Ellie's best interest that she stay with Mackenzie, at least temporarily, until we, including the doctor, know what we're dealing with? I know you have people who are qualified to take care of children with all kinds of traumatic situations. But let's face it, none of us were ready for this. Right now she needs Mackenzie."

Joan frowned, "I don't know. Let me make a call and I'll..."

Chad interrupted. "Are you going to call Wade Proctor?"

She looked stunned. "How could you possibly...?"

Chad said, "I'm sorry, I'm not trying to do any name-dropping, but I happen to have one of the largest charities in the Boston area, called the Jenny Fund."

"You're *that* Chad Hamilton?"

Chad was not only embarrassed but also uncomfortable. "Yes, guilty as charged. My biggest and the most important of our donations are to Hope House, which is a special place for children with many and all kinds of challenges. I meet occasionally with your director and some of his managers, including Wade."

"So, Mr. Hamilton," she said cautiously, "Are you name dropping to impress me or trying to intimidate me?"

Chad smiled, "Which one works?"

"Okay, you can keep Ellie, temporarily, but I'll be closely monitoring your efforts."

Mackenzie said, "Thank you, Joan. You won't regret your decision."

"I'm already regretting it. My posterior could be in the proverbial sling for this."

"Not to worry," Chad said. "As soon as we are done here, I'll make a call to Wade to let him know that I threatened and tortured you, and that because of your graciousness, I'm going to make a personal donation to Hope House in your name."

Joan laughed, "Now we're talking bribery. You'd better quit while you're ahead."

———

"Did you get the job done? Are the Sandersons dead?" the voice said.

"Yes, sir. It was real messy as you ordered. A message was definitely sent. You must hate these people pretty bad, boss."

"I don't even know them."

"Then why d..."

"I don't pay you to ask questions, you idiot. But you did a good job. With the three of them dead, I can move on to the next phase of my plan."

Silence.

"The three of them? There was only the husband and the wife."

"I told you there was a little girl."

More silence.

"Did you check under the bed and in the closet?"

"No, I thought...."

"You thought, did you? The one thing you didn't do is think, you moron! I don't need this. Find that girl and eliminate her, or there won't be a place small enough for you to hide. Got it?"

"Yes, sir."

———

CHAD AND MACKENZIE walked out of the hospital. Ellie was holding tight to Mackenzie's hand. Chad asked, "What now?"

"I think you should take Ellie and me to my condo. She needs to get back to a little bit of normal if that's possible. Then if you don't mind, maybe you could track down some of Ellie's clothes at her home. I don't think it's a good idea for her to go to her house. I think she might immediately start looking for her parents, trying to bring everything back to normal, which is not going to happen."

"Okay, I'll try. Maybe I can get Katie to help me buy her some new clothes."

Mackenzie said, "That would be great. She might like that. After all, a girl at any age likes new clothes."

"I'm on it. I'll be back as soon as I can with clothes and pizza. If she's going to eat, that should do the job."

"Thanks. I love you."

"Love you, too. Just another great day of sailing, huh? I don't know how I get into these situations."

"I think God puts you in these circumstances because you can do something."

Chad said, "Oh please, there you go again, God had nothing to do with this." He paused for a moment. "Really, do you honestly believe that?"

"He led you to me, didn't He?"

"Well if He did, would you thank Him for me?"

"It wouldn't hurt you to thank Him yourself."

"Actually, I do. Got to cover all the bases, you know." Chad wasn't a religious person but he had had some challenges in his life that had brought him to reflect on his beliefs and develop a value system that had sustained him over the past decade.

The grandson of a billionaire who had built an industrial company from the ground up, Chad was the heir apparent to the business and, at age twenty, was at the beginning of his senior year at Harvard in Cambridge, Massachusetts, when tragedy struck. His sister, Katie, and his girlfriend, Jenny, were struck down by a pickup truck while crossing the street. Jenny died, which sent Chad into a deep depression where he disappeared and eventually ended up enlisting in the Special Forces in the Army. That was the beginning of Chad's transformation. Seeing all the death and destruction, he vowed that if he got out alive, he would use his money and status as an influence for good. He also met Kade, who was an operative for the CIA and assigned to Chad's unit as a consultant that knew the areas in Africa. Not liking each other in the beginning, they soon

13

became great friends; and after Chad got out of the service and Kade left the CIA as a burnt-out alcoholic, Chad came to the rescue. He helped Kade set up his own detective agency under the financial umbrella of Hamilton Industries.

Chad's phone rang. He looked at the display, KADE. "Hey, how'd your meeting go?"

"Okay. I'll tell you about it later. I got news from Neal."

"Great! What did he find out about the Sandersons?"

"Actually, nothing."

"Nothing?"

Kade said, "Nothing that would help us. So far they are clean, totally."

"That doesn't make sense, Kade. If you could see that death scene, you'd know what I'm talking about. This was a killing with a message, an execution. Have Neal keep looking."

"Will do. I guess this puts a damper on dinner tonight."

"Yeah, tell Sydney I'm sorry and I promise to make it up to her." Sydney was Kade's girlfriend. They'd met six months ago when he and Chad were trying to save Evans Pharmaceuticals from a hostile takeover. She was a detective with the Natick Police Department and the daughter of Kade's handler when he was with the CIA. Chad, Mackenzie, Kade, and Sydney had been a foursome for the last few months, sometimes choosing to dine at one of the restaurants at Hamilton Towers in downtown Boston. Hamilton Towers was Chad's crowning achievement. His real estate prowess had helped make him the golden boy of Boston, along with his charities that helped many deserving people throughout the community.

Kade said, "I think I can figure something out. Syd and I will muddle along as best we can."

"I'll bet," Chad laughed. "Talk to you tomorrow."

Chad's phone rang just as he was finishing Kade's call. "Hello."

"Chad, it's Ender."

"Hey, buddy, what's up?"

"We've got a situation down here at headquarters."

Chad actually chuckled. "Aw, is the FBI having a challenge? And you called me? I'm flattered. How can I help?"

Ender said, "You can't."

"I'm confused," Chad said. "You have a problem. Then you call to tell me I can't help. What's the problem?"

Ender took a deep breath. "You are!"

CHAPTER THREE

"What?! What does Ken Stout want with me?"

Ender said, "I don't know for sure, but he didn't seem too happy. He said to be in his office tomorrow at 8:00 sharp."

"Oh he did, did he? You tell Mr. Stout I'll be there at around 10:00."

"Come on, Chad," Ender lamented. "Let's not get him all worked up before you even get there."

"Just deliver the message." Chad hung up.

Chad had been sitting in his favorite lounge chair in his penthouse at Hamilton Towers when the call came from Ender. He'd been sitting there, wondering what had happened to the nice, leisurely day that he had planned with Mac; a lovely morning and early afternoon of sailing, followed by an evening of dining with Mac, Kade and Sydney. He looked down at the end table. "Not now, Doug," Chad whispered. Chad had been keeping a journal faithfully for over a decade. His girlfriend at Harvard, Jenny, had convinced him that a journal would enhance his life and, except for a period after Jenny died, he'd been keeping it ever since. He had several volumes that he had grown to cherish. From the very beginning he called his journal Doug, which seemed to personalize it.

"Okay okay," Chad muttered.

Hey, Doug,

I know I just talked to you 2 days ago, but I need to vent, and you're it! Tell me, Doug, am I a magnet for trouble, or just plain lucky? Mac says that God puts me in these situations because I can usually do something about them. If that's true I wish He would trust someone else for a while. I haven't completely recovered from our last escapade. Chad rubbed his chest where he'd been shot six months earlier, nearly losing his life. *I've got a meeting in two days in Montreal with the mayor, then with the architect who's drawing up plans for a new stadium, and then Treat and I have a marathon meeting to make some serious decisions about our baseball team. But then you already knew that, didn't you? And now I get a call from Ender, who says the Regional Director of the FBI is mad and has requested my presence tomorrow. Great! I wonder what that's all about. I don't have any parking tickets in my glove compartment. Oh well, nobody ever said life was going to be easy or smooth, but can't it just pass me by a little more often?*

CHAD SET his journal back down, thinking that at least nothing else could possibly happen. Then his phone rang. Chad started to yell NO when he saw the display, *KATIE.*

"Hi sis, how's it going?"

Katie said, "Never mind about my boring little world. I just got off the phone with Mackenzie. Talk about being in the wrong place at the wrong time! What are you going to do and how can I help?"

"I don't know what I am going to do but you can help by buying some clothes for the little girl, Ellie. She is seven years old and we don't want her to go back to her house. That would be so helpful. Do you mind?"

"I would love to do that for you. How are you holding up?"

"We'll get through this. We always do. So how are things going at Hamilton Industries?"

"Everything's fine, Chad. A few challenges here and there as usual, but nothing as earth-shattering as yours." Katie was Chad's twin sister. Since she was twelve minutes older than Chad, he called her *big sister*. Her short-cropped hair was dark like Chad's and she also had Chad's striking blue eyes. At 5 '11', she was athletic and could be imposing to some of her subordinates, which was sometimes helpful. As President of Hamilton Industries, she had great responsibilities. Hamilton Industries was the largest distributor of industrial cleaning products in New England. Chad had been the president and Katie the vice president; however, two years earlier he stepped down because of all the outside real estate projects, including Hamilton Towers, he was involved in. Chad stayed on as Chairman of the Board but was not involved at all in the daily operations. "So, bro, is there anything else I can do for you?"

"At the moment, nothing. I may have to get the team together soon. I'm not getting good vibes about this trouble. Deep down I get the feeling that there is more to this double murder than we know."

Katie said, "What do you mean? You're not saying that somehow you are involved, other than just literally stumbling on to the Sanderson's boat, are you?"

"No, I'm not. It's just a feeling that I'm getting that things are not exactly as they seem."

"Uh oh. Those feelings of yours usually pan out. I'll wait to hear from you. In the meantime I'll let Lawrence know that we might be meeting." Lawrence was Hamilton's lead attorney, a very good friend of Chad's and a part of the so-called A-Team.

"Thanks, Katie."

As Katie was hanging up the phone, Kade came walking into her office. "Hey, you big gorilla, what are you doing here?" she inquired.

"Stopping by to see Neal, so I thought I'd drop in to see how my little sis is doing." He picked Katie up off her feet, giving her a big hug.

"I'm doing great. Are you here to see Neal about Chad and Mackenzie's situation?"

"Partially, I've already got him working on that. I've got a missing person's case I need his help with."

"Well look what the wind blew in!"

Kade turned around, breaking into a huge smile. "Hello, gorgeous. How's the most beautiful woman in the world?"

"Kade, you are so full of...."

"Now now, Sara. No need to get testy," Kade laughed.

A company or organization always has that person who holds the whole thing together. Sara was that person, the glue that held Hamilton Industries together. She was 50+ years old with stylish grey hair and always looked sharp. Working with the company for over 30 years, she'd known Chad and Katie when they used to run around Hamilton Industries as little kids. She'd wiped noses and tears. Starting out as a secretary, she was now the vice president of operations, knowing every aspect of the business. Putting it mildly, Sara was a beloved institution at Hamilton Industries.

Katie said, "Kade is here to see Neal." She proceeded to tell Sara about Chad and Mackenzie's eventful day.

"My goodness, that's terrible. Is Neal working on any of this?"

Kade said, "He is and another project I'm going to give him."

"Well, good luck, dear boy. I hope things work out."

Katie said, "Me, too. However, I just got off the phone with Chad and he may put the team together for a strategy meeting. I'll let you all know."

———

CHAD AND MACKENZIE were sitting on the couch at Mackenzie's condo, Ellie at Mackenzie's side. They were eating the pizza that

Chad brought. Ellie was staring at the TV but didn't seem to be focused on it. She seemed oblivious to the conversation going on between Chad and Mackenzie.

"What does the Regional Director of the FBI want with you?"

"Not a clue. Ender said he was not a happy camper. I can't believe it. Don't we have enough on our plate right now? Are you going to take some time off from work to take care of Ellie?"

"Yes, I talked to Dad. We got it covered. I've got a great assistant which will most likely make things better without me."

Chad said, "I highly doubt that!"

Mackenzie smiled. Chad loved her smile that seemed to light up the room. He was thinking back to the time they first met. It seemed like ages ago, yet it had been less than seven months. So much had happened in that first month. Chad, Kade, Katie and many others had been put in harm's way as a result of Chad's interest in helping Evans Pharmaceuticals out of their financial trouble. He sat there smiling at her.

"What?" Mackenzie asked.

"I was just wondering if our life together is going to always be like this, one adventure after another."

"Well, if it is, I hope there are a few breaks along the way."

Chad said, "Me, too. I don't think my heart can take too much of this. It's just barely healed from our first escapade." Chad touched his chest.

"To think I nearly lost you before it all began. Don't ever scare me like that again, mister."

"Believe me when I say, *ma'am, I'll do my best.*" Chad sat quietly for a moment. "You know, Ms. Evans, maybe it's time I start thinking about making an honest woman out of you."

Mackenzie said in her best southern accent, "Why, Mr. Hamilton, I declare, are you asking me to marry you?"

"This is not exactly what I had envisioned as the right romantic moment and location. Here we are sitting with a little girl whose parents have just been murdered and have no idea what we're going to do about it. But yes, that's what I'm asking. I've been crazy about you ever since we met that day in your office. You looked like you wanted to do away with me but even then I knew you were something special."

"I did want to do away with you, you scum-sucking raider. But your charm and good looks eventually won me over. YES, I'll marry you." She jumped up and straddled Chad, giving him a long, lingering kiss. Suddenly they stopped, realizing that Ellie was now sitting right up against them, staring with absolutely no expression on her face.

"Oh, Ellie, what's going to become of you?" She removed herself from Chad's lap and took Ellie back to where they'd been sitting. Ellie slid her arm back inside of Mackenzie's.

Chad said, "We'll discuss the marriage thing at a later date."

"Count on it, buddy boy, in the very near future!"

Chad smiled as he got up and walked over to Mackenzie, leaned over and kissed her on the cheek. "See you tomorrow." He patted Ellie on the head. "Bye, Ellie."

"Good luck with the FBI tomorrow morning."

"Thanks, I think."

———

Chad got out of his blue Lexus in the parking lot at Boston's FBI Headquarters. Still wondering what this was all about and getting more annoyed by the minute at the way he was summoned to this meeting, he slowly made his way into the lobby, walking to the front desk. "I'm here to see Ken Stout. I have an appointment. My name is Chad Hamilton."

"I'll let Mr. Stout know you're here, Mr. Hamilton. Please have a seat."

After waiting for 15 minutes, Ender entered the lobby. "Hey, Chad, let's go on up."

As they entered the elevator, Chad said, "What's going on, Ender?"

"You'll know soon enough. Don't worry, Chad Hamilton always lands on his feet, right?"

"Oh, that's real comforting, Ender."

Agent Brimhall smiled.

They walked into a small reception area and walked on by the desk. "Ken is expecting us, Shannon." They walked into Ken Stout's office. He was sitting at his desk. He got up, came around his desk and extended his hand to Chad, "Thanks for coming, Chad. Sorry you had to wait."

"Good thing I didn't come at 8:00." Chad said sarcastically.

Stout let the remark pass. He pointed to one of two black chairs adjacent to his desk, "Please have a seat." Chad sat down as Ender positioned himself in the other chair. "First, let me again thank you for all the work you did in apprehending Peter Strickland. What you and Kade did was next to impossible, but somehow you pulled it off. How's the chest?"

"It's doing okay. Is that why you ordered me here, to check on my health?!"

Stout smiled, "I guess I deserve that. You are only here so that I can deliver a message."

"A phone call could've taken care of that." Chad was still a little put off by all this.

"No, it couldn't." Stout said.

"Okay, I'll bite, who is this message from?"

"It's not a message, Chad; it's an ultimatum from Martelli."

CHAPTER FOUR

CHAD SAT up a little straighter in his chair. "What does Jack Martelli want with me? How does he even know me?"

"Oh, he knows you all right, trust me. He knew all about what you and Kade did six months ago. He also knows about Neal and his aptitude."

"So?"

"So, he let it pass that we allowed you all the slack we did because everything turned out well and he thought that would be the end of it. I actually got a bit of a tongue lashing for giving you the leeway that I did but that's all history. But when you found those two bodies yesterday there were big implications that this could be the beginning of a major drug operation, possibly involving organized crime."

"Again, so?"

"So, he knows that Neal has already been looking into the Sanderson's backgrounds. Our computer guys may not be quite up to Neal's standards, but they're no slouches. And I'd be willing to bet a month's salary that you've already got Kade working on it."

Chad said, "Listen, Ken..."

"No, Chad. You listen and listen good! We are not, and I repeat, we are *not* in negotiations here. You've been ordered by one of the most powerful men in America to back off. To ignore his orders could be suicidal. He has the resources to take any fact in your life and make it look like anything he wants. He told me to remind you that he could put the brakes on your baseball enterprise before it gets off the ground." Stout paused to let what he said sink in. "The Director is coming to town in four days for the very purpose of meeting with you. I'd suggest you take this warning seriously, Chad. You are a great person and do wonderful things with your charities and resources, better than anyone I've ever met. But you're out of your element here. Let us take care of business. We have all the assets and knowledge to get the job done. Do I make myself clear?"

"Quite. So when is this meeting supposed to take place?"

"Saturday morning at 9:00 a.m."

"Saturday, huh? Is that so they can discreetly remove my body from the premises?"

At that statement Ender leaned forward putting his head in his hands.

Stout said as he stood up, "Agent Brimhall, I trust that you will make your friend see the gravity of this before Saturday?"

"Yes, sir."

As Chad and Ender were waiting for the elevator, Chad looked at his friend. "What a bunch of ..."

Ender stopped Chad before he could finish his sentence. "Look, pal, this is really serious. Ken and I know what you and your team can do. But once Director Martelli found out, it had to stop. He had no choice. He can't allow any kind of vigilantism to occur or we'd have total chaos, you know that."

"I suppose so. I guess from now on, we'll have to be more careful."

Ender said, "You still don't get it. Don't be stupid. They have things on you and Kade that could put everything you do in jeopardy." Ender took a deep breath. "They know about Kade's trip to Miami and the sudden disappearance of Peter Strickland's two henchmen."

"There's nothing to tie their disappearance to Kade."

"That's what I'm trying to explain to you. There doesn't have to be. All the Director has to have is the idea of impropriety. With his influence he can take the most innocent act and make it seem like much, much more. Besides, you and I both know that Kade eliminated those two pieces of garbage. Please, Chad, take this seriously and back off."

Chad was silent for a moment as Ender walked with him to his car. "Okay, Ender, you win." Then he smiled. "I guess you know that in our next racquetball session, I'm going to clean your clock."

"In this case, it'll be well worth it."

———

A SHORT TIME after Chad's meeting with Ken Stout, Mackenzie was at the hospital with Ellie for further evaluation with Dr. Worthen, the Chief of Psychiatry. The session went well. At the end Ellie was sitting at a small table in the corner of the office, playing with a children's puzzle, while Mackenzie and Dr. Worthen visited at his desk.

"So what do you think, Doctor?"

"It's way too soon, Mackenzie. The fact that she's not talking worries me. Her brain is obviously in protection mode, not allowing her to fully comprehend what has happened. We, in reality, don't know what she saw or what happened, and we may never know."

Mackenzie said, "Chad figures that since she's alive she must've been hiding somewhere and then after the perpetrators left, she tried to get her parents to wake up. She was covered in blood when we found her on deck. Do you think she knows that they are dead?"

"Somewhere in her mind, yes. But as I said, her brain won't allow her to understand the full impact of this tragedy. It would be helpful if you can get her talking. Maybe ask her simple things about food or TV. Obviously nothing about the murder of her parents."

Mackenzie took a deep breath, letting it out slowly. "Okay, Doctor, I'll do my best. When should we see you again?"

"What Ellie needs is time. If you have any breakthroughs or concerns, do not hesitate to call me."

"Thank you, Doctor. Let's go, Ellie." She immediately got up from the table and made her way to Mackenzie.

Dr. Worthen said, "Any luck on finding her family?"

"No, not yet."

"Good luck," Dr. Worthen said. "Good-bye, Ellie."

———

As they were leaving the hospital Mackenzie said, "How about some lunch, Ellie? Would you like to go to McDonald's and get a happy meal?"

Ellie nodded her head in the affirmative. She seemed to acknowledge the term *happy meal.*

While on their way to lunch, Mackenzie noticed a blue sedan behind her. She knew she was most likely being a little paranoid but was going to be cautious nevertheless. At the first stop she turned right. The sedan also turned right. She saw in her rear view mirror that there were two men in the car. She proceeded on to a four-way stop, pulling into the left turn lane. The sign above posted *No U Turn.* Mackenzie proceeded to make the illegal turn to see what the blue car would do. It made the same turn. Mackenzie's stomach did an immediate flip. She drove to the highway that she had made the original turn on and got back on the highway that was leaving Boston and entering Cambridge. The car followed. She reached for her cell phone and pushed the speed dial button for Chad, put it on speakerphone, and then set it on the seat.

"Hey, Mac, I was just thinking about you."

"Chad, I think we're being followed."

"Where are you?"

"We are just entering Cambridge on Highway 15. We were headed for the McDonald's near my condo."

"What makes you think you're being followed?'

26

Mackenzie told Chad what had happened and what she did.

"It's probably nothing Mac, but it sounds a little suspicious. I was on my way to see you girls so I'm only a couple of minutes away from McDonald's. I'll meet you inside. If these guys are following you I want to lure them inside so we can get a good look at them. Maybe we might get a reaction from Ellie if she sees them."

"Chad, I'm scared."

"I know. Try to stay as calm as possible. I'll see you in a few minutes. Don't worry, Mac. I'm not going to let anything happen to you."

"Promise?"

"I promise. How did things go with the doctor?" Chad was trying to get Mackenzie to calm down.

"It was a good visit. He said that Ellie is going to need time, a lot of time, but that it's too early to know how she is doing."

Chad said, "That poor little girl. No one, especially a child, should ever have to go through that kind of trauma."

Chad pulled into the McDonald's parking lot. "Okay, Mac, I'm here. See you in a minute." He went inside, ordered a coffee and then walked to the farthest booth at the back against the wall and sat down. He pulled out his phone and called Agent Brimhall.

"Ender, we've got a little situation."

"Are you serious? We haven't been out of our meeting with Ken for an hour and you already got something?"

Chad told Ender everything that was going on. "Okay, Chad, there's no time for me to get over there so keep me informed, and please don't do anything stupid or macho."

"Me? Why, Special Agent Brimhall, I'm just a pussy cat and a concerned civilian."

"Right." Ender hung up the phone and smiling, mumbled, "I love that guy."

———

As if on cue, Mackenzie and Ellie walked in as Chad was returning his phone to his pocket. Mackenzie looked at Chad with a relieved smile on her face. "Hey, sailor, do you come here often?"

Chad grinned, "Evidently not often enough. Is that blue Chevy that just parked outside the one?"

Mackenzie looked out the window and nodded in the affirmative. "That's the one. Do you think they had anything to do with Ellie's parents?"

"I don't know. Hopefully they'll come inside so we can get a better look at them. Why don't you and Ellie sit down and I'll go get us some food? What should I order for her?"

"She seemed to perk up a little when I mentioned a happy meal."

"Sounds like a plan. I used to live on Big Mac's in college. How 'bout you?"

"Just a salad please."

"Oh come on, Mac, live a little dangerously. How about a double cheeseburger?"

Mackenzie smiled but still had a worried look on her face. "A salad will be just fine."

As they ate their meal it became obvious that the strangers were not going to come in. Ellie ate most of her meal while Mackenzie sat nervously playing with her salad. She was not hungry at the moment.

Chad took the last bite of his burger. "Oh, that was awesome. I'd forgotten just how good one of those could be."

Mackenzie said, "How can you be so casual about this?"

"Because I was really hungry." Chad could see that Mackenzie was a little irritated about his aloofness. "Don't worry, Mac, these guys are not going to harm you and Ellie."

"How can you be so sure?"

"Because I'm going to ask them politely to leave you two alone, and then, I'm going to pick a fight!"

CHAPTER FIVE

"You're going to what!?" Mackenzie looked horrified. "You and Kade do that a lot, don't you?"

"These guys won't expect me to come up to them. Here's what I want you to do. Wait for about one minute after I go out, then take Ellie to your car and drive to your condo. I'll meet you there in a few minutes."

"But, Chad..."

"Don't worry, Mac, I know what I'm doing. I'll see you in a few." At that, Chad got up and walked out the door.

Chad walked straight towards the blue car. When he was about ten feet away, he smiled and waved. He maneuvered to the driver's side where the window was down. "How ya doin'?" he said.

The man behind the wheel said nothing.

Chad said, "Can I help you guys? You look lost. I know these roads can get a little complicated in this area. Where are you headed? I know this area very well. By the way, my name is Chad Hamilton."

At that moment Mackenzie and Ellie came out and walked directly to her car. The man in the passenger seat said, "Get lost, Hamilton."

Chad said, "Okay but first," he reached into his pocket and pulled out his phone. "I need a picture of you two since we're now friends." Before they could react the camera on his phone clicked.

"Mister, you have no idea who you're messing with." The man speaking saw that Mackenzie was pulling out of the parking lot.

"Don't even think about it!" Chad said as he saw the driver move to start the car. "You're not leaving just yet. That lady leaving is very important to me and I know that you definitely know who the little girl is since you were involved in her parents' murder." At that statement both men froze. "Good, now that I have your attention, here's what you two are going to do. You're going to start your car, leave this parking lot going in the opposite direction of the car you were following. Then you're going to call your boss and tell him that you've been made and are no longer relevant. Here's what I'm going to do; I'm going to send your license number and your picture to my friend at the FBI. I'll just bet you are already in their files and that they'll be more than happy to invite you over to their place for a nice talk. Won't that be fun?"

Chad went silent for a second then said, "You guys have a lot to think about. You may go now."

The driver looked over to his passenger who evidently was in charge. He nodded and the driver started the car and slowly made his way out of the parking lot. Chad watched until they were out of sight, and then took a deep breath. He immediately called Mackenzie to let her know that everything was okay and he'd see her in a few minutes.

———

"Do you think that those guys were following me because of Ellie?"

"No doubt about it," Chad said. "I saw it in their faces. Whoever is behind this doesn't want any loose ends. We're going to have to be even more careful from here on out. I've got a meeting with Kade and Neal in about an hour to talk about the showdown this morning at

FBI headquarters. We'll definitely discuss your incident and come up with a plan."

"About that meeting; what's going on?"

"Nothing much. The Director of the FBI has warned me to back off of the Sanderson murders, or else."

Mackenzie said, "Or else what?"

"No big deal. He'll just destroy my life, my career and my family if I don't."

"Oh that's all, is it? I hope you listened and are going to comply."

Chad smiled. "Of course I am, Mac. What else can I do?"

Mackenzie took a long look at him and sighed. She knew how much Chad didn't like ultimatums or threats, no matter who they were from. She knew that he and Kade were very good at getting out of trouble and how resourceful they could be. But the FBI! "Oh, Chad, you know I trust you with my life, but maybe this is one fight you don't want to get involved in. You've got those big meetings tomorrow in Montreal concerning your baseball team. That should be enough adventure, don't you think?"

"Yes and about that, you were going to come with me."

"Under the circumstances, I think it would be better if I stayed here with Ellie."

"Nonsense. I think the trip would do her good and get her mind off of things. Since the Sandersons had that nice boat I'm sure Ellie has flown before. It'll do you both good and until Kade, Neal and I can get our teeth into this situation, I want you two close to me."

"Maybe you're right."

"Of course I'm right," Chad said with a sly smile. "Talk to Ellie about it later when I'm with Kade and Neal. See if you can get a response out of her about flying in a great big airplane."

———

KADE AND NEAL were waiting in Chad's penthouse at the Hamilton Towers when he arrived. Kade had the code to Chad's private elevator so they had made themselves comfortable and were working on Kade's missing wife case. They weren't having much luck. So far Judy Wainwright hadn't used any credit cards. She had withdrawn four hundred dollars at an ATM.

"I figure she can't get far on that."

"Who?"

Kade looked in Chad's direction as he was coming off the elevator. "I'm working on a missing wife investigation, the one I told you about earlier."

"Oh yeah, I remember. Any luck so far?"

"No, not yet, but Wonder Boy here is working on it."

Neal smiled and said, "I'll get her. You just need to give these magic fingers a little time."

Chad said, "So what are you going to do when you find her?"

"I'm not sure. Her husband has sleaze-ball written all over him. I wouldn't trust him past my nose. Says he's in the import/export business, which always sounds a little shaky at best. First we find this Judy Wainwright, and then I'll determine my next move."

"Did you say Judy Wainwright?" Chad sounded excited.

Kade looked stunned. "Don't tell me you know her?"

"Nope, just thought I'd ask."

Neal burst out laughing as Kade glared at Chad, a disgusted look on his face.

Chad started laughing too as he said, "Gotcha! Sorry Kade but I've had two stressful days and I needed to lighten my mood. I really hope you find this lady soon."

"Got her!" Neal shouted.

"No way," Kade said.

Neal said, "Why do you doubt me, Mr. Kincaid? Haven't I always come through?" Neal pretended to pout.

"You're right, young man. I don't know how you do it. Where is she?"

"I'm not one hundred percent, but I think you'll find her at the Comfort Suites in Framingham."

"Why?"

"First I checked the location of the ATM where she withdrew the four hundred. I figured she left in a hurry and the first thing she most likely thought about was where to stay. The closest hotel to the ATM is the Comfort Suites, only one block away."

"Okay," Chad said, "I'll bite. How could you possibly know that she would be there and how could you find out?"

"The answer to the first part of your question is I didn't know so I checked six different hotels in the vicinity. The second part gets a little more complicated. I hacked into each hotel's computer and looked for people staying more than one night. Once I narrowed it down to multiple nights, I checked for women who registered. Of course I looked for Judy Wainwright even though I was pretty sure she wouldn't register in her own name. When I didn't find her, I searched for a name that might be made up and, voilà, there it was."

"There what was?" Kade asked.

"Mary Smith."

"Mary Smith sounds made-up, Neal, but don't you think that's a bit of a stretch?"

Neal smiled, "I'm not finished yet."

Chad looked at Kade, "He's not finished yet. What else do you have, Mr. Computer Whiz?"

"She just withdrew another two hundred dollars at the same ATM twenty minutes ago." Neal folded his arms and looked at the two guys. They just stared at him.

Kade said, "You're the man. Is she still registered at the hotel?"

"Yes, for two more nights."

"Great, I'll stake out the hotel in the morning and see if she's our gal. Wainwright gave me a current photo of her. Outstanding job, Neal!" Kade turned to Chad. "You need to give this boy a raise."

"You're pretty free with my money, aren't you? Just so you know, I already have."

"So," Kade said, "what's been so stressful about today?"

Chad proceeded to enlighten them about his day, beginning with his meeting with FBI Regional Director, Ken Stout, and his warning from the FBI Director. Then he told them about his encounter with the two bad guys at McDonald's.

"What a day," Neal said. "No wonder you're feeling stressed."

Kade said, "Sounds like fun to me. So, Mr. Hamilton, what are you going to do? Or should I say, what are *we* going to do?"

"First, those two guys are definitely tied to the Sanderson murders. Until Neal can get us more information, we need protection for Mac and Ellie. I'll be with them tonight and I'm taking them with me to Montreal tomorrow. Once we get back tomorrow night, I want them to have around the clock protection."

"Done," Kade said. "Now, what about this FBI situation? Are you going to take the Director's threat seriously?"

"Definitely. We need to be much more careful." Chad's lip slowly curled to a full-blown smile.

Kade smiled. "That's my boy. So what can Neal and I do?"

Chad proceeded to unfold his plan.

CHAPTER SIX

ELLIE SEEMED to enjoy the ride in the Hamilton corporate limo on the way to the airport. Even though she still didn't speak, it was apparent that she was beginning to adapt to her new situation. It had only been three days. She clearly would improve, but to what extent no one knew. She, Mackenzie, and Chad, boarded the Hamilton corporate jet and took off for Montreal, which would only take about an hour in the air. Chad had made arrangements for a rental car, so the threesome headed to city hall where Chad would be meeting the mayor for a short conference and some publicity photographs.

In their first meeting four months earlier, Chad and Mayor Richard Cousineau had discussed the challenges they were facing financially as a city, what went wrong the first time the Expos baseball team was there, why they left, and the work they had done to get another major league team back in Montreal. Also attending that first meeting was Treat Robinson, the President of Chad's team and Chad's boyhood best friend. Ever since high school they had talked constantly about someday owning a major league baseball team, and now, it was actually happening. To say they were excited was an understatement of gigantic proportions.

Of course, starting a new major league baseball team had many challenges. One of the biggest issues was where they would play. The Expos, as they were called previously, had played at Olympic Stadium, a multi-purpose stadium built for the 1976 Olympics. Although it served its purpose for the Olympics, structurally it was a complete disaster. One of its biggest problems was a Kevlar roof that leaked from the very beginning. On March 14, 2014, the New York Mets and the Toronto Blue Jays played an exhibition game at Olympic Stadium. It rained during the game and the roof leaked so badly they nearly had to cancel the game. The list of problems went on and on. The Big O, as the stadium was called, later became known as The Big "Owe" as the projected cost of the stadium went from an estimated 300 million dollars to the actual cost of over 1.5 billion. In order to be awarded a new major league franchise, the city fathers of Montreal had to almost guarantee that the stadium problem would be solved. So Chad was doing his best to help Montreal with the projects that were going on to improve the stadium. He was part of the committee formed to enhance the area around the stadium. He also hired his own architect to help. Chad's expertise in real estate was an enormous help to the committee.

After the meeting with the mayor, Chad and Treat went to the local mall to check up on Mackenzie and Ellie. They met at the food court for lunch. Mackenzie gave Treat a big hug. "Treat, I'd like you to meet Ellie." Chad had filled Treat in on Ellie's sensitive situation on their way to the mall.

Treat knelt down on one knee. "Hello, Ellie," he said, extending his hand. Ellie frowned and stepped back, moving halfway behind Mackenzie. Treat was expecting as much. "I hear you like pizza? That's my favorite. How about we get some right now?"

Ellie said nothing, but nodded her approval.

Chad said, "We've been eating a lot of pizza these last couple of days. Treat, why don't you go over to that Mexican place and get us some burritos or something that excites your palate and I'll go get Ellie a big slice of pizza?"

While they were eating their food, Chad's cell phone buzzed. "Hello, this is Chad."

"Got a message for you, Hamilton. We want to talk to the little girl. No harm will come to her or you and that pretty girlfriend of yours. We just need to clarify a few things."

Chad didn't want to alarm Mackenzie so he got up from the table, signaling that it was an important call. "You have me at a disadvantage, my friend. You know who I am but I don't know who you are. Is that fair?"

"Someone with your, and the little girl's best interest in mind."

"I highly doubt that," Chad said. If nothing else he wanted to try and remove the danger from Ellie and Mackenzie. "Besides, when I found Ellie on the Sandersons' boat, I found her hiding in the pantry. She was in the galley where her father probably put her when he saw danger coming. She did see her parents after what you and your partner did to them and is severely traumatized. She can't even speak and knows nothing." Here came the hook, "But I do."

"What are you talking about, Hamilton?"

"I found a tape recorder under the bed and it was still running. I have no pictures but I do know exactly what happened. I'm sure the FBI with all its sophistication and expertise will have no problem with voice recognition. I've got it locked in a safe place in my penthouse and as soon as I get back from Montreal tomorrow, it's going straight to the FBI. I also have voice recording on my phone. What do you want to bet that your voice and the voice on the tape are one and the same?"

"Okay, smart boy. We'll see you soon."

"Looking forward to it." Chad hung up before anything else could be said, and then made his way back to the table.

Mackenzie said, "Who was that?"

"Mayor Cousineau. Nothing important. It's all about the details."

———

THIRTY MINUTES LATER, Treat and Chad met at the office that Chad had leased, while Mackenzie and Ellie spent some fun time at the park. Before they got into the business at hand, Chad made a phone call to Kade. He told him about the threatening phone call he'd just received.

Kade said, "I understand you wanting to take the heat off Ellie, which also makes things safer for Mackenzie, but are you nuts?! You just put a bull's-eye on your back."

"It seemed like a good idea at the moment. Anyway, you're going to protect me, aren't you?"

"I've been doing that a lot lately. I'm guessing you have a plan."

"Of course I do. I've had two encounters with these guys and twice they have screwed up. I don't imagine whoever's in charge is happy with them. Desperate times call for desperate measures. Here's what I think they're going to do and, if they do, here's what I suggest you do." Chad told him his idea.

"You know, that just might work. I'll get right on it."

"Of course it'll work. See you tomorrow."

———

"NOW WHAT DO WE DO? If we tell the boss that Hamilton has made us and he's got a tape to prove it, we're dead."

"You're right. We've got to get that tape tonight before he gets back tomorrow. Let's find out where Hamilton lives and get that tape."

———

BY NINE O'CLOCK THAT NIGHT, they had a plan and found a way to get in to Chad's penthouse. They found out who the maid was, grabbed her and the key to the back entrance of Chad's apartment. Then they tied her up and put her in a storage area. Since it was evening they weren't too concerned about anyone finding her until morning. They took the elevator to Chad's floor. "Have you got the key?" Walt asked. The man in charge worked the key, unlocking the back door. "Okay Mitch, let's get started. Since we're in the kitchen we'll start here." They tore the kitchen apart, opening every drawer and cupboard. They checked the refrigerator and freezer, and anything else they could think of. When they were done, the kitchen was a mess.

"Nothing," Walt said.

"This was just the first room. Let's try the living room." Mitch pushed on the swinging door that led to the living room. Much to their surprise, two men were sitting casually on the sofa smiling at them.

"Come on in, boys," Kade said.

Both said nothing, stopping in their tracks.

"Cat got your tongue? Oh, I know, it's because you don't know me," Kade said. "I'm Kade and my friend here is Ender, but you can call him FBI Special Agent Andrew Brimhall."

Ender waved with his left hand while revealing the revolver in his right. "Why don't you two sit over there in those two chairs?"

They sat down, still silent. They'd been caught red-handed and knew it.

"Did you gentlemen find the tape yet?" Kade asked.

The apparent leader, Mitch, said, "We aren't saying anything. We want to talk to our lawyer."

Ender said, "That's a wise choice. You're going to need all the legal advice you can muster. However I would like to give you what I view as some of your options if you cooperate with me, so I would advise you to listen carefully."

"Here's what we got so far," Kade said. "First, breaking and entering. My guess is that you and your buddy are two or three-time losers and that alone is going to put you away for a few years. Next, Chad Hamilton set you up. We knew you were coming and that you needed a way to get in. Chad's personal maid that you tied up is safe and sound ready to testify against you two. Now, let's get to the real issue. You are here because we have voice proof on tape that you two brutally murdered the Sandersons."

"Now," Ender said, "you two are going away for a long time, most likely for the rest of your lives. I know you guys are very low on the food chain in your organization. We still don't know why and that's where you come in. I've been authorized by our regional director to cut a deal but only if I get some answers before we leave."

Kade said, "I would imagine that the head of your organization is not pleased with your work so far. In fact, I think if I were you, I'd be more worried about your safety and physical well being from your business associates."

"If you give us everything you know, I can offer you safety and incarceration at a facility where you can receive protection."

"Anyone can get to us once we're in prison. That's no guarantee at all."

"It is if you never go to trial."

"What?" Mitch said.

"You admit to your part in the crime, tell us everything you know, and we'll send you to a prison right now. It'll be like a witness protection program. You'll be in for a long time but you'll be alive and well. It's better than the alternative."

Mitch said nothing for a minute, and then said, "No deal, I'll take my chances without your humanitarian pitch."

Ender smiled and said, "Okay boys, it's your funeral." He and Kade stood up. "You two down on your knees and put your hands behind your backs"

"Wait!"

CHAPTER SEVEN

W

ALT SAID, "I'll tell you everything I know."

"Shut up, you idiot!" Mitch screamed.

"No, Mitch, not this time. He's right. We're dead men as soon as the organization can get their hands on us." Mitch remained silent for a moment, then shrugged his shoulders as he made a decision.

Mitch said, "You guarantee no trial and we go to a facility where we will be protected?"

Ender nodded. "That's the deal. Let me make it clear. It will most likely be for the rest of your lives but you will be safe."

Mitch paused a moment, then said, "Okay, you got a deal."

"All right." Ender pulled out a recording device. "I'm recording this." He first stated all the parties that were in the room, and then stated the deal that he had offered Mitch and Walt in order that they would feel secure that Ender was on the level.

Ender then had them state their names.

"Good. We are here to discuss the murder of Alex and Janette Sanderson. Mitch, what was your involvement?"

Mitch then related how he and Walt received orders to follow the

Sandersons for a few days. Their phone had been tapped so they knew in advance the day they were to go sailing. Then they rented a boat that had the capability of speeding far above the capacity of the Sanderson's boat. He then gave the brutal details of the execution. It made Kade's stomach turn. He'd seen plenty of this kind of brutality in war but it never seemed to get easier. The death and killing was why he finally left the CIA.

Kade then asked, "Who ordered the hit?"

"I don't know," Mitch said truthfully. "We never know who gives the order."

"Yes, but the order had to come from someone you know in your own little organization."

"He wouldn't know any more than me."

"We'll be the judge of that." Ender said, "It's one step closer to the top. Name?"

"Bruce Atoll."

Ender said, "I'll take your cell phones."

"Won't do you any good. They're throwaway burn phones. When we talked to Atoll he was using a burn phone too."

"Okay, we may have more questions later but that'll do for now. I need you to stand up and put your hands behind your back." Ender cuffed them and they headed for the private elevator, which took them down to the main lobby. Chad's elevator was in an area off to the side of the main entrance. With Ender holding the arm of one of the men and Kade holding the other, they exited the building. Their first indication that something was wrong was when Mitch collapsed. Before he hit the ground Ender and Kade heard the sound of a rifle shot in the distance. Kade instinctively tried to jerk Walt to the ground, but it was too late. When Walt landed his eyes were already open in death. As Kade and Ender dropped to the ground with their guns already drawn, the shooting stopped. After a few seconds Ender saw that Kade was looking off in the distance.

"What are you looking at?"

Kade said, "That building over there."

"That's five hundred yards away, Kade. Who makes a shot like that?"

"I do. That's why we didn't hear the shot until after the first guy was already hit."

People near the entrance of Hamilton Towers were beginning to react to the scene. Some were in total shock. Others were silently staring, not knowing what to do. Ender jumped up and pulled out his FBI badge. "I'm Special Agent Andrew Brimhall. I need all of you to go inside to the lobby and wait there. We will need to get a brief statement from each of you. Please be patient and we will get to you as soon as possible."

Thirty minutes later several agents were at the scene, including a forensic team. Also in attendance was Ken Stout, the regional director. After hearing Ender's report, Stout narrowed his eyes. With Kade in earshot of them he barked, "What part of our meeting with Hamilton yesterday did you not understand?"

"After Chad called Kade earlier today, he called me. I had to make a quick decision and determined this was the best way to go."

Stout said sarcastically, "How about now?"

Ender said nothing.

Stout looked at Kade. "Your buddy Hamilton has a meeting Saturday morning in my office with the Director. I'd suggest you be there too."

Kade smiled, "Love to."

"Brimhall, I want you in my office in the morning at 8:00 sharp."

Ender nodded but again said nothing.

As Kade and Ender were walking away, Kade said, "Sorry, buddy, Chad and I aren't winning you any brownie points with your boss, are we?"

"It's okay, I've been in worse situations, but I am glad that the FBI is only domestic and not foreign. At least I can't be banished to Siberia."

"Good point."

———

THE NEXT MORNING after returning from Montreal, Chad called Kade. "Any news after last night's shooting?"

"Not yet," Kade said. "I haven't had a chance to talk to Ender yet. He's at FBI headquarters getting his butt handed to him."

"Does this mean I have to keep letting him beat me at racquetball? I was just starting to get my full strength back."

"Yep, at least another six months worth. He didn't seem too concerned. Said it wasn't anything he couldn't handle. On a more positive note, I did get a personal invitation to your meeting with the Director on Saturday morning."

"Great! I'm looking forward to it. Shall I bring doughnuts and coffee?"

"Might not be a real good idea with the mood that he's going to be in. Of course, we could slip a Prozac in his drink. It might have a calming effect on him."

Kade said, "You're probably right. Just between you and me, I'll be packin'."

"Oh, nice. You plan on shooting the director of the FBI?"

"I do if he hurts my feelings."

Chad chuckled to himself. "So, what's our big-time private investigator up to today?"

"I'm staking out the Comfort Suites where Judy Wainwright is staying. She hasn't come out yet but I'm hoping it's soon."

"Are you sure it's her?"

"Yeah, our boy somehow hacked into their cameras and I got a good look at her. It's her all right. I'm not sure what I'm going to do when she comes out. I've got a bad feeling about her husband."

"Well, I'll tell you, Kade, those feelings we get sometimes have saved our lives. I recommend you proceed with caution."

"Way ahead of you, Cupcake." Kade ended the call and immediately dialed a familiar number on his phone.

"Hi, handsome. How's the stakeout going?"

"You of all people should know how much fun stakeouts are, Detective Nichols. I really have to go to the bathroom!"

Sydney laughed. She had spent many hours on stakeouts for the Natick Police Department. Her father, who had handled Kade when he was with the CIA, had helped her learn the value of enduring patience and calm persistence. Once the Evans case had been solved, Kade and Syd, as he called her, spent most of their down time together. Although Kade acted casual about their relationship because that was just his style, he was crazy about her. The feeling was mutual.

Kade said, "What are you up to?"

"I'm knee deep in paperwork. We completed a sting operation on a theft ring we've been working on for months. We finally got them last night so I'm riding pretty high today. I don't really mind the paperwork this time."

"Good girl! I... oops, gotta go. My prey is finally coming out of the hotel. See you tonight."

Judy Wainwright slowly strolled to her black Mazda and drove away. Kade kept his distance while following her. It didn't take long until she pulled into the parking lot of a Denny's Restaurant. She walked inside and was led, at her request, to a far booth. She sat with her back against the wall so she could see out the window at the parking lot. Kade went to the counter, took a seat and ordered a cup of coffee.

Judy ordered a club sandwich and a Coke and began eating when Kade approached her. "May I join you?"

She said, "No, you may not."

Kade threw down his card that identified him as a private investigator. Judy immediately stiffened and looked extremely pale.

"Did my husband hire you?"

Kade sat down and said, "Yes, he did, but I haven't had good feelings about him since we met. Would you like to tell me why?"

She began to shake uncontrollably. "Do you want to know why I left him? Do want to know why he's trying to find me?"

"That's why I'm here, Judy. Can I call you Judy?" Kade extended his hand. "My name is Kade. Your husband says he's sorry. He knows he's been a jerk and has neglected you. He wants to make amends. He's even booked a cruise for the two of you next month."

Judy said nervously, "I would imagine he plans on taking that cruise right after my funeral."

Kade was taken aback by her statement and said nothing.

"Arthur wants me back all right." She paused. "So he can kill me!" She began crying.

Kade let her sit there for a moment. He handed her a napkin. "Are you going to be okay? Tell me why you believe he wants to kill you?"

"Arthur is involved in many things that I don't understand. When I have confronted him on some issues that seem unusual or even illegal, he either clams up and ignores me, or gets violent, telling me it's none of my concern."

"He admits to me that he has shut you out and swears he's going to change."

Judy smiled. Speaking in an almost cautious tone she said, "Some things can't be changed."

"Like?"

"Murder."

For a second time in less than five minutes Kade was caught totally off guard. "What makes you think he's involved in murder?"

"I don't think, I know. Last week he had two men in his office. I don't usually visit his office but on this particular day I needed his signature on a document for the bank. I was in the outer office. His door was slightly open, about an inch. He was having a conversation with two men. I couldn't believe what I was hearing. He was giving the men instructions about cleaning-up after they kill some people on a boat."

Kade froze with her last word. "Did you hear the name of the people they were going to kill?"

"Yes, but I don't remember,"

Kade said, "Was it Sanderson?"

Her face went pale. "I believe it was. How could you possibly...?"

Before Kade heard the ping from the window, Judy Wainwright's head snapped to the side as she slumped to the floor.

CHAPTER EIGHT

KADE INSTINCTIVELY DOVE to the floor, at the same time reaching behind his back, grabbing his Glock. It was obvious to him that she had been shot. While lying on the floor waiting for the next shot he looked over at Judy. He crawled over and put two fingers to her neck, feeling for a pulse. He was relieved to see that she was alive, but unconscious. The bullet wound looked like it wasn't a direct hit, but nasty nevertheless. He looked around and saw that everyone looked shocked and confused. Kade shouted, "Everyone down on the floor. This woman has been shot from outside. I'm calling the police now."

Kade hit 911, told the operator what had happened. Then he slowly moved up and looked out the window, surveying the parking lot and everything in the vicinity. He told everyone to stay down until the police arrived. He then tried to reassure them that the shooter was gone and that everything would end soon. Then he dialed Chad on his phone.

"What's the matter, Kade, you miss me already?"

"I sure do. Would you like to know why?" Kade then told Chad what had happened and his conversation with Judy Wainwright, right up to the time she was shot.

Chad said, "I don't know about you, but in the words of Yogi Berra, *I'm starting to feel déjà vu all over again.* I don't believe in these kinds of coincidences."

"Nor do I. Listen, Chad, I'm heading to the hospital with Mrs. Wainwright so I can make sure she's okay and see that she gets around the clock protection. Then I'm going to pick you up and we're going to pay a visit to Arthur Wainwright and get some answers."

"I'll be waiting."

"Looks like we got ourselves into another one, doesn't it?" Chad said.

"What do you mean, *we?*"

"Ah, Kade, you know I wouldn't neglect you in one of my adventures. Admit it; the old adrenaline is moving pretty fast through those veins of yours, isn't it?"

Kade smiled. "Guilty as charged. This sure is bizarre though. What are the chances that you'd be out there on the water, find two dead people, and I'd be working on my own case that ends up tying into yours?"

"I'd say one in a million."

"Except when Chad Hamilton is involved. Then I'd lower those odds to about one in ten."

"We do seem to attract trouble, don't we?"

"There you go with that *we* again."

———

WHEN THEY ARRIVED at Wainwright's building and were almost inside, Chad said, "So what made you doubt this guy in the first place? Just some of that old instinct of yours?"

"You got it, buddy. I will tell you this, he better come up with some good answers or I'm liable to wring his neck. That's why I called you and had you come with me, to maybe save his life."

Chad said, "Too late." Arthur Wainwright was lying on the floor in his outer office, a pool of blood underneath his head with what appeared to be a bullet hole in his left temple. "I'm assuming that this is Wainwright?"

"That would be a correct assumption." Kade and Chad stood silently over Wainwright's body. Kade said, "My my, the plot thickens. What are you thinking?"

"Honestly, I'm thinking about how much fun our meeting in the morning with the director of the FBI is going to be."

"Oh, you mean the one who ordered you to back off the Sanderson murder case?"

"That would be the one."

"That's tomorrow's challenge. Right now I'm going to do the normal thing and call 911 for the second time today, and then call Ender and give him the gory details."

"In the meantime, let's see what we can find out by looking around."

"Whoever is behind this, they seem to be one step ahead of us all the time."

As they combed Wainwright's office it was obvious that it had been stripped. All computers and anything electronic were gone. "This was definitely a professional job," Kade said. He took the phone and unscrewed the mouthpiece. "Got a bug here." He slipped it into his pocket and then wrote down the phone number. "We'll see if Neal can do anything with this. I've also got his cell phone number. I'm guessing that there's some kind of hidden bug or surveillance equipment hidden here somewhere. Maybe they were in a hurry and didn't remove it either."

They began looking in the usual places, under the desk for a sound apparatus, behind pictures for cameras, and then anywhere a camera or video recorder wouldn't be seen. Kade looked up and saw a smoke alarm. "Hmm ..., maybe up there." He grabbed a chair and removed the cover. "Nothing. This place is clean."

They waited for the police to arrive, told them as little as possible, and then met Ender about an hour later at a coffee shop in Cambridge.

"I swear," Ender said. "I hope there's good coffee where the Director is going to put you two."

Chad actually smiled. "Oh, I think once he gets to know the real me and sees Kade's charm, he'll most likely throw us a going away party first, don't you agree, Kade?"

"It's the least he can do."

Ender groaned. "Director Martelli will probably throw the book at you two and it'll miss and hit me right between the eyes!"

———

THE NEXT MORNING CHAD, Kade and Neal were sitting in the lobby at the Boston FBI headquarters at 8:00 a.m. Chad decided to bring Neal and his computer along just in case; for what, he had no idea. After a few minutes Ender came in and escorted them up to Ken Stout's office.

Upon entering Stout's office, Chad had the feeling one might have going into the principal's office in high school. Stout and FBI Director Jack Martelli were sitting in the two chairs that were across from Stout's desk. They had been turned around with their backs to the desk, facing a large black leather couch. Martelli pointed to the couch. "Sit down, gentlemen."

Chad said, "So much for introductions."

"Cut the crap, Hamilton. We all know who everyone is. This isn't a social gathering. If you don't come up with the right answers in this meeting, you three will rue the day you were born. I have the resources at my fingers to make you three disappear permanently, so I'd choose your words carefully." He noticed Kade was smiling. "Is something funny, Mr. Kincaid?"

"I was just wondering. You must have a tremendous amount of agents ready to pounce on us. Funny I didn't see very many while we were walking in, because, you know what it would take to best Chad and me? How would you explain over twenty dead agents? Actually, I guess you wouldn't, would you? You'd be one of those twenty."

"Well, well, Mr. Ex-CIA operative and world class sniper. Did I touch a nerve?"

"Not at all. Just wanted you to know that your little intimidating speech got nowhere with me, and even less with Chad."

Martelli glanced at Chad, who smiled as he shrugged his shoulders. "All right, boys, let's get to it. I found out only recently of your involvement over six months ago with the Evans situation. Your intrusion into that little fiasco left a trail of dead bodies. You're lucky I didn't know about that because, had I known, I would've put a stop to it immediately." He sent an accusing glance over at Ken Stout. "Since you were lucky that everything turned out okay, I've let it pass."

Chad said, "You mean right up to the part where Peter Strickland escaped at the courthouse steps while in the custody of the FBI?"

"These things happen, Hamilton. The FBI isn't perfect, but we are very good at what we do and don't need amateurs like you interfering in our operation."

"We have no intention of getting involved with the FBI. Perhaps you think I was out on my boat just looking for trouble?"

"Trouble does seem to find you, doesn't it?"

"Kade and I were just discussing that two days ago. To answer your question, no, I don't look for trouble. This Sanderson circumstance couldn't come at a worse time. Maybe you've heard. I've been awarded a baseball franchise in Montreal and I've got less than a year left to field a team. It's been my dream for most of my life. I want out of this as much as you want us out of it!"

Martelli said, "Well you've certainly got a funny way of showing it. In the last four days since I ordered you to back off, you confronted the guys responsible for the murder of the Sandersons. Then, while in Montreal, you lied to them to set up your own sting, and then they get shot and killed before we had a chance to interrogate them. Is that what you call backing off?"

"Those two were following Mackenzie and the daughter of the Sanderson's. They initiated the contact. I lied to them to take the heat off of the girls and lure them to my apartment at the Hamilton Towers. Every step of the way I was in contact with Ender."

Martelli asked, "Who is Ender?"

"Agent Brimhall," Ken Stout answered.

"Ah yes, Agent Brimhall. I'll be dealing with him after our little get together here."

"Why?" Chad asked.

"Don't worry about him, mister. Do you know what I could do to you? One phone call to the commissioner of baseball and your owner-ship of that Montreal baseball team is history. I could also make a phone call to my friend at the IRS and bring down your charity you call the Jenny Fund, which I know is dear to your heart. And that's just the beginning. I can tie up Hamilton Industries for years and create havoc with all your real estate business in Boston. All that good you do right down the toilet. What a shame." Martelli smiled smugly and folded his arms.

Chad said nothing for a moment. Then he sat up and said, "But you're not going to do that, are you, Michael?"

CHAPTER NINE

MARTELLI CAME up out of his chair. "What did you call me?"

"Michael Capeletti. Your grandfather's name was Guido Capeletti, who, as you well know, was a Mafioso hit man in Italy back in the 1940's and 50's."

Martelli was now standing over Chad. "Where did you come up with such nonsense? You can't sit there and intimidate me with your lies."

"Intimidate?" Chad said. "You're the one standing over me with a red face. I'd say that you are the one who seems a little flustered." Chad looked over at Neal, Neal handed him a file. "Let's see, Michael Cappelletti, born in 1962; parents, Tony and Maria Capeletti. They were murdered execution-style in 1966. To protect you, your mother's sister and her husband took you in, and through some very carefully forged documents, changed your name to Anthony Martelli. You then officially became their son." Chad began looking through the folder. "This is interesting, a sealed juvenile record for Anthony Martelli. I wonder what's in there?" He paused. "Whoa. Tony, Tony, you naughty boy." Chad sat still for a moment. "Listen, Mr. Director, I could go on, but I don't think you want that. I admire the work you do and what you are trying to accomplish with the FBI. You're a good man, Tony, and I believe that I am too. But, if I go down, you go down, and that would be tragic. So why don't you get to the point and tell me why we are really here?"

Martelli was quiet for a second and then sat back down. "Ken, ask Agent Brimhall to join us."

After Ender grabbed a chair and sat down, all eyes returned to Director Martelli. Slowly he began to smile. Addressing Ken Stout he said, "I like them. They're everything you said they were, and more." Neal looked a little confused, but Chad and Kade were calm. "Sorry about the little charade boys, but I had to be sure."

"Sure about what, sir?" Chad queried.

Martelli said, "When I saw the extent of what you did six months ago, I was at first upset at what I deemed your interference. But when I delved further into your participation, I realized that you three did some extraordinary things. What you did when your sister was kidnapped, Chad, was a thing of beauty. Coming up with a plan like that with your own sister the victim, well, let's just say I've never seen anyone with that kind of personal pressure on them, perform the way you did."

"Trust me," Kade said. "I've seen him do that time and time again."

"Don't be modest, Kade," Martelli said. "The way you found that hit lady Carter was pretty heads-up."

"That's true," Kade said modestly.

"Oh, don't be so egotistical about it. I could still throw the book at you regarding the disappearance of two known enforcers in Miami. They've simply vanished from the face of the earth."

"Sorry, sir, I have no idea what you're talking about."

Martelli smiled, "Right. Then once you found Carter, putting the hit out on yourself to lure her in was a gutsy move."

Chad said, "It was a crazy move!"

Kade smiled, "Worked, didn't it?"

"Yes it did," Martelli said. "That's the point I want to make. You gentlemen not only have rare talent and abilities, but you can also, shall we say, bend a rule or two. The FBI can't do that."

Chad said, "So what are you saying?"

"Once in a while, I'd like to call on you Chad, and your team, to help us with a particularly difficult case. Occasionally we at the FBI are at a standstill because of lawful restrictions that help the criminals more than us."

Chad countered, "You want us to break the law. Is that what you're saying?"

"Not at all. Like I said earlier, sometimes you boys bend a few rules to get to the truth. But you always do it for the right reasons."

"Which makes everything okay?"

"You're starting to sound like a lawyer, Chad. The bottom line is that I want you three to be my own special task force to be used on specific occasions that would require, let's say, your special abilities."

"Who sanctioned this?"

Martelli said, "No one but me. The only ones that will ever know about our little team are us. Your liaison will be Agent Brimhall. His partner, Agent Sean Gibbs, won't even know. In fact Sean is receiving his transfer orders as we speak. Agent Brimhall will become a special projects coordinator. There will be no record anywhere of our relationship. If we get found out, nothing would happen to you, but my career will be over. In my files I will have the three of you as consultants, but that's it. It's all on me."

Chad handed Martelli the file folder. "I guess I won't be needing this."

"Neal, you are amazing. How did you get this information? Never mind," He chuckled, "I don't want to know. Our own computer experts here in Boston say you're the best they've ever seen."

"By the way, sir, ignore that $100,000 deposit to your account yesterday. Neal will see that it is removed by tonight."

The director's mouth dropped as he stared at Neal, who smiled sheepishly. "How...." Martelli stopped. "Forget it, I withdraw the question." He looked at Chad. "So, do we have a deal?"

"Do you have a case in mind?"

"Yes," Martelli said, "the one you already are working on, the Sanderson murders."

Chad said, "I'd like a minute alone with Kade and Neal."

"Fair enough. Ken, why don't you, Agent Brimhall and I get a cup of coffee?"

"I'd like Ender to stay, sir." Martelli stared at Ender and then said, "Fine."

After the two men left Ken Stout's office, Chad moved to the chair Martelli had been sitting in so he could look straight at Kade and Neal. "What do you think?"

Kade smiled, "Sounds like fun to me. But I have to be up front, it's been my experience that if something goes wrong, the guys in the field usually take the fall."

Chad nodded then looked at Neal.

"I'll do whatever you and Kade decide," Neal said. "You know I'm behind you 100 percent."

"Thanks, Neal. Okay, Ender, can I trust Martelli?"

Ender said, "I think so, but I'd cover your butt at all times. What Kade said is true. If anything hits the fan, you boys will most likely take the fall."

Chad sat quietly for a minute. "Ender, you want to invite them back in."

After Martelli and Stout sat down Chad said, "Here are my terms."

"Whoa, son," Martelli bellowed. "You don't set terms, I do!"

Chad got up and said, "Okay, we're through here. Let's go, boys."

"Wait a minute, Chad," Martelli said. He looked over at Stout. Stout smiled and gave him a look that said *you better listen to him.* "What terms?"

"First, you put in writing over your seal that we are acting as

consultants to the FBI on projects deemed important by the Director
and that there will be no funding or fees involved."

Martelli said, "Not a problem. We're going to set up an offshore
account for you that can't be traced."

"You're not hearing me, Tony. No money, period. If somehow
what we are doing becomes public knowledge, I want there to be no
show of impropriety at any level. If we need to fly somewhere, we
will take the Hamilton corporate jet. We will spend our own funds.
Our involvement will be completely voluntary every step of the way.
Got it?"

"Got it. Anything else?"

"Actually, no. There may be some details as we work together. As
soon as I get the original letter stating that we are consultants only,
we'll begin. Actually," Chad said, "we've already started, but then
you know that, don't you?"

Martelli laughed. "Yes, Chad, that I do. Because of the brutality
of the Sandersons' murder, this case is receiving national attention.
So, where are you boys at on your investigation? Before you begin, I
might let you know that we discovered a fifty thousand dollar deposit
in Alex Sanderson's account. Looks like his hands are dirty after all,"
Martelli said smugly.

"Not really," Neal said sheepishly.

Martelli gave Neal an annoyed glance.

Chad said, "We know about the fifty thousand, sir. It's not even
relevant."

Martelli looked puzzled.

"Look at the date and time the deposit was made."

Martelli opened a folder he pulled from his briefcase.

"You'll see that the deposit was made within hours of the Sanderson's murder. The guy behind all of this most likely made the deposit
as an afterthought to throw me off track."

"Don't you mean throw the FBI off track?" Martelli said.

"Do you believe in coincidences, Director?" Kade asked.

"Almost never."

"Neither do Chad nor I."

Martelli tilted his head but said nothing.

"On the same day that Chad discovered the Sandersons, I was hired by an Arthur Wainwright to find his wife." Kade proceeded to explain to Martelli all that had happened and how Wainwright's wife had been shot yesterday at the restaurant. "She overheard her husband discussing the hit on the Sandersons."

Martelli said, "Is she going to be okay?"

"Yes," Chad said. "Kade and I don't believe in coincidences either. We went to Wainwright's office last night and found him shot to death. That's when we called Ender."

"So," Martelli said, "you think this has something to do with you guys?"

"We know it," Chad said.

"Do you know who?"

"Only the one person it could be."

Martelli sat quietly staring at Chad when the light bulb in his head lit up. "Peter Strickland."

CHAPTER TEN

CHAD SMILED. "THE ONE AND ONLY."

"So the most wanted man in America is behind this. Why?"

"Revenge."

Kade said, "Chad ruined everything that Peter had worked for. He won't stop until Chad is destroyed. But before that he'll want to punish Chad."

Martelli sat silently, folding his arms. "Peter Strickland. That's quite a stretch."

"It is, Tony," Chad said. "But it makes perfect sense. He had it all and we destroyed it. I don't have proof yet but my gut tells me it's him."

"I agree with Chad," Kade said. "Isn't that why you want us to cut through all the smoke and get to the truth?"

"Yes I do. You gentlemen have my complete confidence and approval. Just keep me informed through Agent Brimhall, that's all I ask."

Chad said, "You got it."

"There is one last thing," Kade said.

Director Martelli let out a deep breath. "What is it, Mr.

Kincaid?"

"Can I have that chocolate donut? I'm starving!"

———

"Nice of you two to let me know that you think Peter Strickland is behind all of this," Neal said.

"We wanted to surprise you," Chad teased. "Actually we just came to that conclusion last night. We aren't sure."

Kade said, "But it sure smells like him."

They were riding in Chad's car after the meeting with Martelli at FBI headquarters. "What I need you to do, Neal," Chad said, "is to see if you can find Peter."

"Talk about finding a needle in a haystack," Neal groaned.

"More like finding a needle in 100 haystacks." Chad said. "Follow the money. We weren't able to get to his Swiss account, so start there. Also, that fifty thousand that suddenly showed up in the Sanderson's account had to come from somewhere."

Neal smiled. "Well, Chad, you know my motto: the extremely difficult I can do, the impossible will take a little longer."

"Atta boy, kid," Kade said. "Peter won't know what hit him."

———

Chad dropped down on Mackenzie's couch. "Hi, Ellie."

Ellie, who was sitting at the end of the couch said, "Hi."

A startled Chad glanced over at Mackenzie, who was smiling. "She's starting to open up a bit. Nothing spectacular but every little bit helps, right?"

"Absolutely. Have you relayed this good news to Dr. Worthen?"

"Yes, he is very encouraged by this. Would you like some more good news?"

Chad continued to smile. "I'm always open for good news."

"I received a call from the social worker, Joan Calhoun, about an hour ago. It seems that Ellie's next door neighbor has been gone on vacation. They were out of the country and just returned yesterday. They weren't even aware of what happened to the Sandersons. Their daughter Kayla and Ellie are best friends. They're on the way over to pick up Ellie. She's going to stay with them and see if it works out. They have already indicated a willingness to adopt her."

Chad stared at Mackenzie. "How do you feel about it?"

"I know what you're thinking, Chad. I'm okay. It's true, I've become attached to that precious little girl, but I want what's best for her. Besides, I think there is going to be room for an Aunt Mackenzie and Uncle Chad in her life, don't you?"

"Absolutely," Chad said as he walked over to Mackenzie, leaned over and kissed her. "I love you, Aunt Mackenzie."

"And I you, Uncle Chad. I've packed her clothes that we bought her and added a few little things."

"I'll bet you did." Chad laughed.

The doorbell rang. Mackenzie walked over to open the door with Ellie tagging along. As she opened it, Ellie immediately saw Kayla and screamed with delight. The girls began playing and doing what little girls do while her parents smiled at Mackenzie.

"I guess you know who we are. I'm Norman Johnson and this is my wife, Sharon."

"I'm happy to meet you. I'm Mackenzie and this is Chad."

Chad extended his hand to Mr. Johnson. "It's a pleasure to meet you, Norm. I'm sorry it has to be under these circumstances."

"Me, too. I understand you were the ones that found Alex and Janette. Can you tell me what happened?"

Chad started at the beginning and gave them as much detail as he could without telling them of his present involvement.

Johnson said, "Do you think Ellie is in any kind of danger? We dearly love that little girl but I fear for my own family's safety."

Chad said, "None whatsoever. I've been in contact with the FBI and we are 100 percent sure that whoever is behind this has no interest in Ellie." He didn't elaborate on the fact that he was now the target of the bad guys.

Johnson seemed satisfied with Chad's comments.

"We'd love to have you stay for dinner. I think that would help Ellie with the transition."

"That's very kind of you," Sharon Johnson said. "Can I help?"

"Thank you," Mackenzie said, "but I've ordered pizza which has been Ellie's favorite staple for the last few days."

"Mmm, pizza," Kayla said.

"Looks like we've got a winner," said Norm.

———

Two hours later, Chad and Mackenzie were sitting on the sofa together and alone. "I miss her, Chad. Is she going to be alright?"

"Yes, she is, and so are you. She needs time but some things she'll never get over. Still, children are resilient. She'll adapt in time to her new environment and family. What you need right now is a change."

"Not now. I need to spend tonight feeling sorry for myself. Maybe tomorrow."

The doorbell rang. Mackenzie said, "Oh no, who could that be tonight?"

Chad said nothing as she walked to the door. She looked through the peephole, then turned and looked suspiciously at Chad, who smiled sheepishly. She opened the door. Standing there with big smiles on their faces were Kade and Sydney, Chad's sister Katie, and Mackenzie's father, Sam.

With a smidgeon of a smile, but not saying a word, she opened the door wide and gestured for them to come in. Her father was the first to give her a big hug.

"Hi, Munchkin," he said. "It's been ages since I saw you so I thought I'd drop by to see how you are. Imagine my surprise at running into these nice people just outside your door."

"Yes," said Mackenzie, "What a surprise."

"That's quite a coincidence," Kade said. "Syd and I were in the area and thought we'd drop by too. Imagine that?"

"Imagine." said Mackenzie skeptically.

"Okay, okay," Katie said. "We've been had, but when Chad called..."

Mackenzie said, "Oh when Chad called, huh?"

"Oops," Chad said.

Mackenzie sighed, and then smiled. "I'm glad you're here." She looked at Katie. "What's in the bag?"

Katie said, "Guess?"

Mackenzie said nothing but then smiled. "Moose Tracks."

Katie laughed, "You remembered!" When Katie had been kidnapped six months earlier, after the ordeal was over, Chad had showed up at Mackenzie's condo with ice cream; Moose Tracks to be exact.

Kade held up another bag. "And I brought some bubbly. So let the party begin!"

After an hour of laughter and storytelling, Sam Evans said, "So, Chad, now that you're out of this last dangerous incident in your glamorous life, I guess it's back to baseball. I'll bet you are happy about that."

"I know that I am." Mackenzie said. "Finally some peace and quiet."

Chad threw a look at Kade. Kade nodded back. "Um, that's not entirely true."

Mackenzie's head jerked in Chad's direction. "Which part? Is that what your meeting with the FBI Director was about? What did he want? He doesn't expect you and Kade to solve this murder, does he?"

Chad said, "To answer your last question first, yes, he does want our help on this one."

"But why? They didn't like you guys involved even when it was personal. What could make them want you mixed up in this case?"

Kade said, "Because this one is also personal."

"You two aren't making any sense. The last case became personal when Peter Strickland turned all his efforts on destroying Chad. But that situation was solved and you two got him." Mackenzie sat silently for a moment and then almost in a whisper said, "But then he escaped."

"That's right," Kade said.

Sam looked a little confused. "What does the past and Peter Strickland have to do with the murder of those two innocent people?"

"Maybe nothing," Chad said. "But there are some coincidences that lead Kade and me to think that Peter is right in the middle of this and I'm the eventual target."

Katie said, "But you could be wrong."

"Not likely, sis. We're proceeding on the assumption that we are right. The good news is that we're working with the FBI and Ender is the liaison between us."

Kade said, "Neal is getting all the information and technology that the FBI has and is at this moment beginning the process of finding Strickland. So until we resolve this, you are all going to receive around-the-clock protection."

"When will that start?" Mackenzie asked.

Chad replied, "About an hour ago. In addition, Kade is having tracking devices installed on your cars. And if you already haven't done so, put Kade and me on speed dial so you can get to us immediately."

"Anything else?" Katie asked.

Chad said, "No. Kade, Ender, Neal, Sydney and I are meeting tomorrow morning to brainstorm and come up with our strategy. I've also invited Victor Steele to join us."

"Victor Steele," Sam said. "What a difference six months make. To think that he was out to destroy you, Chad, because of something that wasn't even true."

"He's a changed man all right," Chad said. "Do you know that he started a charity that helps veterans with missing limbs and other disabilities caused by war? He donated one billion dollars to get it rolling. It's named The Robbie Steele Foundation, after his son."

"Robbie gave his life to save Chad and me and several others," Kade said.

"Anyway," Chad said, "tomorrow it begins. But tonight we enjoy each other's company."

CHAPTER ELEVEN

Do you believe in luck, Doug? Good or bad? I can't believe the bad luck I'm having, all because of one person, Peter Strickland. I'm meeting with a few people tomorrow and hope we can come up with a definitive plan that we can put into place immediately. Finding Strickland is going to take tremendous effort on our part. I think we are up to the challenge, don't you?

But first thing in the morning, baseball! I'm meeting with Treat to make a couple of decisions regarding our field manager and a general manager. I've got a couple of ideas and I know Treat feels the same way about his recommendations. I'll be glad when that's all we have to worry about. Is that ever going to happen?

———

CHAD'S MEETING with Treat ended at 10:30 in his office at the Hamilton Towers, which was on the floor just below his penthouse. It was adorned with all kinds of baseball memorabilia. Chad was extremely proud of it. It was nicely decorated with a smart touch of informality, which Chad preferred. At 11:00, the meeting regarding Peter Strickland was about to begin. In attendance were Kade, detective Sydney Nichols, Neal, agent Andrew "Ender" Brimhall, Victor Steele, Mackenzie and her father, Sam. Mackenzie and her father were invited at the previous night's activity.

Kade said, "How did the meeting with Treat go?"

Chad smiled, "Great." He seemed to want to delay what they were about to discuss for as long as possible. "We are trying to fill a couple of major positions in the organization as soon as possible."

"Have you got a manager yet?" Victor asked.

"Not yet, but we have someone in mind. I can't tell you who because we haven't approached him yet, but his initials are Skeeter Lefleur."

"What's a Skeeter Lefleur," Kade asked.

Mackenzie said, "He's a man that would be perfect. He has a tremendous amount of managerial experience at both the major and the minor league levels." She looked at Chad. "So you and Treat decided to go with him?"

"We did. We're hoping his outgoing personality and experience will win over the players and fans the same way Casey Stengel did back in 1962 when he managed the New York Mets in their first year of existence. They were awful but the fans loved them and Casey was a big part of it."

Chad said. "And Skeeter is also French which will make him an instant hit with the fans. Treat is actually meeting with him this afternoon so mum's the word."

Kade looked at Mackenzie, "So when did you get all this baseball knowledge?" he teased.

"I have a pretty reliable source."

"Moving right along," Chad said. "We'll talk baseball later over lunch. For now let's get to the business at hand. You all know why we're here. Kade and I have a strong feeling that Peter Strickland is behind these murders with yours truly as his final target. Anyway, we're going to proceed on that assumption. My first objective is to have all of you under the umbrella of our protection. If you haven't already noticed, you all have a shadow that will be near you at all times. We also have my sister Katie, our parents, and our grandfather under constant security."

Sydney said as she looked at Ender, "Is the FBI involved or are you here unofficially as a friend? From what I can tell already, Chad seems to be in charge."

Ender said, "I would be here as a friend, but in this case, the FBI is totally in charge of this investigation," he paused, "with Chad as the lead."

"Okay," Sydney said, "now I'm completely confused. The FBI doesn't put civilians in charge." She stared at Kade. "What's going on, big guy? Why do I feel like I'm the only one in the dark here?"

Ender said, "I'm not at liberty to tell you completely, but suffice it to say, in this case, Chad has been given authority from a source we can't reveal, to be the lead on this case."

Sydney sat quietly for a second. "And you could tell me more, but then you'd have to shoot me?"

Kade said. "Don't worry, Syd, I got your back."

Syd gave him a sarcastic smile and then nodded her head.

———

"ALL RIGHT," Chad said, "now that we're all clear on this, let's see where we are." Chad and Kade took turns sharing everything that had happened since the time that Mackenzie and Chad discovered the Sanderson's boat.

When they were finished Chad asked, "Any questions so far?"

Syd said, "I can see why you think this goes back to Peter Strickland. So, how do we find him?"

Chad nodded to Neal. "Since Arthur Wainwright seemed to be handling things on this end of the operation, I'm going to dissect every part of his import/export business. We also have his cell phone. That should give us some good leads."

Kade said, "And the fact that he is dead leads us to think that Strickland knows that Wainwright could in fact lead us back to him. He definitely doesn't want that."

"Or maybe he does."

All eyes turned to Chad as Ender said, "You want to explain that, Mr. Hamilton?"

"Love to. First let's review what we know about Peter Strickland." Chad proceeded to open up Peter Strickland's life, including the early years when he was Paul Stevens, the years in and out of foster homes, and his meteoric climb to become the boss of one of the most violent and successful crime organizations in Miami. Then he discussed his rise to stardom in the Boston area as Peter Strickland, the golden boy that turned out to be too good to be true.

"In every facet of his life he was in total control and never failed. That's over twenty years of near perfection."

Kade said, "Then in a period of weeks, you came along and destroyed it all."

"Exactly. He wants me in the worst way."

"But he wants you to suffer first," Ender said. "Which means hurting everything and everyone that is important to you."

"That's why protecting my family is priority one. I think he wants me to continue looking and reel me in gradually until we eventually meet for the final showdown."

Kade said, "The old game of cat and mouse."

"Exactly. What he doesn't know is that this is a joint venture with the FBI and if he is out of the country, which I'm reasonably sure he is, we will also have the cooperation of the CIA and all other agencies worldwide. Peter will be sure he is controlling and orchestrating the whole scenario while all along we will be the ones managing the final outcome."

Sam Evans said, "It all sounds good until something goes awry."

Ender said, "Something always goes awry but that's expected and we will be as ready as we can."

"I hate this!" Mackenzie said.

"We all do, Mac. That's why we've got to end this fast and as best we can. Neal, do your best to find this scumbag. As I said, I think he wants us to find him so look for clues that will do just that. The key is Wainwright. Kade and I are positive that his business was illegal. Ender was able to obtain his phone records, so start there. Find out where the bulk of his phone calls were. Once we know that, Kade, Ender and I will see what we can find out at the other end of those calls."

Mackenzie said, "You mean go wherever that is?"

"Yes, we will need to do some on-site investigating of our own. Then we will proceed from there. In the meantime, everyone watch your backs. Even though we have protection for everyone it won't hurt to keep your own set of eyes watching over your shoulder." Chad paused in thought. "Okay, anything else that we need to discuss?"

"Yes, there is."

All eyes went to Victor Steele. "As you all know, I wasn't the poster child for Good Samaritan of the Year up until six months ago."

Kade said, "Your point being?"

"Rules didn't mean anything to me. Strickland will get as dirty as he has to in order to accomplish his objective; I always did. You can't compete with that."

Chad said, "Frankly, Vic, that's why you're here, to give us that perspective. It's why we have the full unofficial, and I emphasize *unofficial,* authority of the FBI. Kade and I aren't going to do anything immoral but we don't have to play by the rules either. We get to use Ender's resources, but we do whatever it takes to bring Strickland down, and I mean anything."

"What happens when you find him, and you and Kade are facing him? Do you turn him back over to the FBI? Will he be extradited back to the USA? What about the threats to your family from then on?"

Chad said, "Kade and I have discussed this at length."

Sam asked, "And?"

"And, it's time to end this meeting," Chad said. "Besides, I've got a more important matter to attend to tomorrow."

"What's that?" Victor asked.

"Grandpa!"

CHAPTER TWELVE

VICTOR SMILED, "I realize I'm old enough to be your father, but calling me *grandpa* is a little..."

"No, no!" Chad laughed. "My grandpa is getting married tomorrow." Everyone except Victor knew Chad's grandfather. Chad told him about his grandpa and how he had been the biggest influence in his life, particularly during his early teenage years. Although Chad loved his parents and had a fairly normal relationship with them now, it wasn't always so. When Chad was a boy, his grandfather was turning over the reins of Hamilton Industries to his son, Chad's father. As a result, Chad's father was always busy and, because of this, Chad spent a lot of time with his grandfather. After Chad's quick exit from Harvard his senior year and his stint in the Army three years after that, he had renewed his relationship with his grandpa.

Chad called his grandfather every week on Sunday like clockwork. As much as he loved him, his grandfather's affection and love for Chad ran even deeper. He was so proud of Chad and what he was accomplishing in his life that sometimes he thought his heart would burst with pride.

Chad said, "Grandpa and Alice are getting married at 1:00 at my parents' home."

"You mean at the Hamilton compound," Kade teased.

"And I'm the best man!" he said with pride, ignoring Kade's comment.

"That's wonderful," Victor said. "Have they known each other long?"

"About two years. We were at a restaurant in Springfield following a Rebels baseball game. Our manager, his wife, and I invited Grandpa to come with us. At the table next to us was Alice with her daughter and son-in-law. I guess Grandpa liked what he saw as he immediately started talking to them and after a few minutes was flat out flirting with Alice. And what's worse," Chad laughed, "she was flirting right back. Come to find out, she was a widow and he'd been a widower for years. And the rest, as they say, is history. Victor, we'd love it if you would join us. And bring Midge." Midge was Victor's secretary or as what Chad and Kade used to call her, the secretary from hell! But that's another story.

"Thanks, Chad, but that sounds like a very special family affair. We'd only be imposing."

Kade said, "Robbie was family, you would be more than welcome."

"Hear, hear!" Chad said.

———

"WHAT A PERFECT DAY FOR A WEDDING," Mackenzie said. "A beautiful blue sky sprinkled with a few puffy white clouds."

"I couldn't agree more, Mac," Chad said. "And may I say you look beautiful." Mackenzie was wearing a pale lavender knee length sheath. Her only jewelry was a pair of pearl earrings and an ivory bangle, bracelet. She had her hair pulled back at the nape of her neck with those delicate loose curls framing her face, the way he loved.

"You don't look so bad yourself, mister." Chad was all decked out in a pale grey dinner jacket with a powder blue shirt and a dark grey bow tie, the same as his grandfather. "Why thank you, ma'am. Nothing is going to spoil this great day."

"Oh, Chadwick!"

Chad groaned, "I spoke too soon. Heaven help me." He called out, "Over here, Mother."

Chad's mother was right out of the book *Gone With the Wind*, a real Southern belle. Chad's father had met her in Savanna, Georgia, on a college spring trip when he was twenty years old. It was love at first sight. He loved her and she loved his money and status. She had to be the center of attention always and truly loved it. All parties and social events had to be under her direction. This wedding was no exception.

"Chadwick, the flowers have not arrived. They were due an hour ago."

"I'm sure they're on the way, Mother. I'll make a call to be sure."

"Thank you, dear." She started to say something else when one of the workers caught her eye. "No, no, not there!" she yelled. "The first row of chairs starts at the front of the..." Her voice faded as she sprinted over to the member of the staff who looked wearily at Mrs. Hamilton. Chad raised his hands to his temples and glanced over at Mackenzie who was laughing.

Mackenzie said, "So where are the bride and groom?"

"My guess is they're hiding somewhere where Mother can't find them until it's time to begin." Chad looked at his watch. "Fortunately that should be in about an hour and a half. I'm going to find Grandpa. I'll see you in a few minutes."

"Okay, I'm going to see if I can help Katie. Your sister has been amazing today. While your mother thinks she's running the show, Katie is really the glue that's holding it all together."

"Katie is definitely the strong one in the family."

"Funny, she says the same thing about her twin brother."

———

"Hey, Grandpa, how's our bridegroom doing?"

"Couldn't be better, my boy. I'm the luckiest man on the face of the earth. I'm going to marry the woman I love and the grandson I adore is my best man."

"Ah thanks, Grandpa. You know what I've been thinking about all morning?"

"You mean besides baseball?"

"No baseball today," Chad laughed. "I've been thinking about all those great fishing trips you and I took while I was trying to grow up. Sometimes I wish we could go back and do it all over again."

"You can't always go back completely, Chad, but it would be kind of fun taking one of those trips again, just you and me. When your dad was a boy, I was so busy trying to save a small but growing business that he and I hardly ever got alone time. When I saw it happening all over again with you, I was determined not to let it."

"And I loved you for it and I'm sure Dad did too, even though I'm sure he was a little envious of our time together."

"Like I said, my boy, you can't go back and change things, but you can make amends by doing a better job going forward. How about a trip with the three of us?"

"I'd like that, Pop," Chad's father said as he strolled up to the two of them. "Today is a good day for making changes for the better."

Chad said, "Then it's a deal. When you and Alice get back from your honeymoon, I'll clear my schedule for a few days and we'll do it. No excuses."

———

"Alice you look beautiful," Mackenzie said. Alice was tucked away in one of the rooms off the living area.

"Why thank you, Mackenzie. You just make sure you aren't anywhere near me out there or all eyes will be on you instead of me."

"Not hardly, Alice. You are glowing. No one is going to upstage you today."

Alice looked radiant. She had found her dress in the first shop she went to, and was so happy. It was exactly what she had imagined when she thought about her wedding dress. The ivory satin A-line with the round neck and elbow length sleeves in antique lace was perfect. The cameo necklace that her grandmother left to her complimented her dress to perfection and made it all the more special. She cut from her own garden some of her prized pink hydrangeas and Mackenzie wrapped the stems in ivory satin ribbons that matched her dress.

Alice blushed. "Would you like to see what I got Chad as a wedding present?"

For a second Mackenzie was startled but then remembered that Chad was Chadwick Beauregard Hamilton III, and his grandpa was the original. "Yes Alice, I'd love to."

She went to a small decorative desk against the wall, opened the drawer and pulled out a small box, and handed it to Mackenzie. Inside was a striking Rolex watch.

"He won't wear a watch. He is always running late. Says he doesn't want time to go too fast. Read the engraving on the back. Mackenzie turned it over. *To Chad, with Timeless Love, Alice.*

"Oh Alice, it's wonderful," Mackenzie said tearfully. "He's going to love it."

Alice said, "Maybe you should take it out to him right now so he'll be on time!"

PASTOR McELROY HAD BEEN a long-standing golf buddy of Chad's grandpa and would be performing the ceremony. He, Chad's grandpa, and Chad stood under the archway in the middle of the lattice that surrounded the area by the pool in the backyard. The violinists played a charming ballad as Alice walked slowly towards them, arm in arm with her son-in-law. When they were a few feet from the three men, Father McElroy said, "Who gives this woman to be married?"

"Her daughter and I do," said her son-in-law Robert. He then hugged Alice and handed her over to Chad's grandfather, who was beaming.

They faced Pastor McElroy with Chad on his grandpa's right and Alice's daughter on her left. He smiled at the two lovebirds. "What a glorious day. I've been looking forward for so long to bring together these two youngsters." There was laughter throughout the crowd. "Marriage is a covenant not to be taken lightly. I am so proud as a friend and an ordained minister to unite these two best friends in marriage. Before I begin, can anyone here give just cause why these two beautiful people should not be united in marriage?"

Chad's grandfather turned and looked sternly at the congregation, as if to say *don't even think of it!* There was another ripple of laughter. Pastor McElroy then continued to give advice and counsel, exhorting them to be faithful to each other and then brought some more chuckles when he said he was going to skip the part about having children and raising a family together.

"You've both done well in that category so I'll just say *continue on!* Now if you'll both take each other by the right hand, we will proceed."

He looked sternly but with a twinkle in his eye at grandpa. "Chadwick Beauregard Hamilton, do you take Alice Christine Dinato by the right hand and promise to love, honor, and cherish her, forsaking all others, as long as you both shall live?"

Without hesitation he said, "And forever, I do!"

He looked tenderly at Alice. "Alice Christine Dinato, do you take Chadwick Beauregard Hamilton by the right hand and promise to love, honor, and cherish him, forsaking all others, as long as you both shall live?"

Her tears were flowing, "I do."

"As part of this ceremony, Chad and Alice will now exchange rings." Chad's grandfather turned to Chad who reached into his pocket and brought out the rings. His grandfather took the ring and faced Alice. Father McElroy then said, "Chad, place the ring on Alice's finger and repeat, 'With this ring, I thee wed.' "

He tenderly slipped the ring on Alice's finger and in a hoarse voice said, "With this ring, I thee wed."

Alice then followed the same instructions placing the ring on his finger and repeated, "With this ring, I thee wed."

Pastor McElroy's smile was wide as he said, "As an ordained minister of the Commonwealth of Massachusetts, it is my pleasure to pronounce you man and wife. Chad, you may now kiss your wife." He gently kissed Alice and they both began quietly laughing as Pastor McElroy turned them towards the audience. "Ladies and gentlemen, it is my pleasure to introduce to you Mr. and Mrs. Chad Hamilton." The guests broke out in clapping and cheers.

———

THE RECEPTION and gala that followed can only be described as epic as Chad's mother was now in her element. After a beautifully catered dinner, a twenty-piece orchestra played while all danced and had a wonderful time. Towards the end, Alice and Chad's grandfather had changed into their street clothes and were preparing to leave. Chad's grandfather was in excellent health, but at eighty years old, he was feeling the effects of a long day. Chad hugged his grandpa and promised a great fishing trip when he returned. He turned to Alice and gave her a big hug, picking her up off the ground. "You take care of this man for me. He is and always has been the light of my life." Then he whispered to her, "I couldn't be happier for you both; welcome to the family."

As the newlyweds got into the limo that was taking them to the airport, Chad was standing next to Kade. "It's been a great day. I wish it could continue but I guess tomorrow it's back to business. Hopefully we can start tearing down Wainwright's company and come up with some answers and a plan."

"I know," Kade said, "but right now I'm still hungry. How 'bout some..." Kade stopped dead in his tracks.

"What? Kade, what's wrong?"

"Our security. We've missed something. I can feel it."

Chad said, "I don't know what. We have guards all around the perimeter of the house and had every delivery vehicle searched as they came in. I think the CIA background in you is just on high alert. I, for one, am glad you're here." As their eyes swept the premises they both froze in unison.

"The limo," Kade screamed, sprinting towards the vehicle that was slowly pulling away from the curb. The limo stopped abruptly when Kade was only ten feet away with Chad right behind. Chad's grandpa stepped out onto the curb. Kade seized him while Chad dove into the limo, grabbing Alice and yelling at the driver to get out.

Seconds later they were all clear of the vehicle. Chad's grandfather and Alice were visibly shaken. Grandpa said, "What in the world are you two doing?" By this time a crowd of onlookers was surrounding them.

Chad said, "It's okay, folks; false alarm. Please go back, have some refreshments and continue having fun." Chad turned to his grandfather, "Sorry, Grandpa. Kade and I realized that we had checked everything security-wise except the limo. I'm sure it's nothing, but we'd like to keep you and Alice around for a few more years, so we had to be sure. What made you stop the limo and get out?"

"I forgot our passports. Can't leave the country without those, can we?"

"No, you can't. Why don't you two go get your passports and Kade and I will check out the car?"

"Okay, my boy. Better safe than sorry."

"Exactly."

Kade took off his coat, and pulled the latch that opened the hood. He looked around but didn't see anything. "Clear."

Chad opened the trunk but didn't see anything suspicious. He then pulled out a blanket and slid it on the ground beneath the undercarriage. Scooting under the limo he instantly froze.

"Found it."

Kade quickly maneuvered under the car next to Chad. "Whoa! That's enough to blow this entire area and half the mansion."

"I don't see any timer," Chad said. "Looks like it's controlled by a remote. Can you disarm it?"

"I think so. It doesn't look complicated. I'm sure whoever has the remote is somewhere along the route or at the airport ready to push the button."

Chad said, "Right, otherwise we'd all be dead now."

"I'll go get my tool kit out of my car while you get everyone into the back yard, just to be sure"

"I'll see if I can get everyone back there without causing any alarm."

"Good luck with that. Everyone is staring at us."

"It'll be my finest hour. You just make sure you don't cut the wrong wire." Chad went silent and then said, "Kade."

"Yeah, buddy."

"I almost lost my grandpa. We've got to stop this psycho!"

"We will and don't give me any crap about bringing him in for trial. When we find him..."

"I know. Dead meat."

CHAPTER THIRTEEN

THE NEXT FEW hours were unsettling but Kade and Chad were able to pull off the charade without his parents or grandpa and Alice knowing what had just happened. Katie, Mackenzie, Sydney, and the security team were the only ones privy to it. Chad and Mackenzie drove the newlywed couple to the airport while Kade and one of his security guys drove the limo. Kade sat in the passenger seat hoping to spot the man with the detonator. It worked. Just as they were pulling up to the curb at the airport, Kade spotted a man that looked out of place. Instinctively, Kade jumped out of the car and sprinted straight for the man. Startled, the man pushed the button on the detonator. When nothing happened he automatically pushed again as he turned to run. By then Kade was on top of the man, threw him to the ground and rolled him over face down. His security guard, Owen, came running up and pulled out a pair of handcuffs.

"You shouldn't play with toys, pal, especially at the airport," Kade said.

"What are you talking about?" the man said.

"Oh, I think you know." Kade checked the perpetrator's pockets, pulled out a cell phone and put it in his own pocket.

A couple of airport security guards came sprinting up.

Kade said, "This gentleman was about to blow up that limo over there. Call the authorities and have them call Ken Stout at FBI headquarters in Boston."

"Is he a terrorist?" one of them asked.

"No, just a dirtbag trying to ruin a wedding. Make your call and everything will be okay." While Owen held the man down, Kade called Chad, who was dropping off his grandpa and Alice at a private part of the airport. Chad was taking no chances. He was having the corporate jet fly them to their honeymoon destination.

Chad said. "Any luck?"

"Got him." Kade said triumphantly. "We're in front at the American Airlines terminal."

"Be there in five. Great work!"

"Thanks, Chadwick the third. Do I get a raise?"

"How about another piece of wedding cake?"

———

A few minutes later Chad was holding the cell phone that Kade had confiscated. "I'm sure whoever is at the other end of this is waiting for a confirmation that the deed is done." He smiled at Kade. "I guess I shouldn't keep him waiting." He had determined that this was a burn phone and couldn't be traced, but he'd let Neal see if he could work some magic on it.

Chad hit redial. After one ring a voice came on the phone. "I hope you have some good news for me?"

Chad said, "I do. It's done."

The voice said, "Excellent, there's going to be a special bonus added to your already exorbitant fee, but well worth it. Hamilton will be reeling and devastated by this."

Chad couldn't believe his ears. It was Peter Strickland. He knew his voice very well. He said, "One more thing."

"What's that? "Strickland said.

"We found the bomb. My grandfather is safely tucked away somewhere. I don't think I need to tell you that I will find you, and when I do, I'm going to kill you."

"Chad, you are amazing! I'm so impressed. Let the games begin!" the phone clicked off.

Chad stared at the phone and then looked at Kade.

Kade said, "Let's get back to the mansion, make sure everything is secure, and then find this guy."

———

"Is that who did this?" Katie said as she walked towards them. Her eyes were red and she looked like she hadn't slept in days, even though it had been only hours. She was shaking uncontrollably. "I can't believe we almost lost them. What if Kade hadn't thought of the limo?"

"But he did, Katie. Everything is going to be okay. To answer your question, yes, it was Peter Strickland."

"Then you find him. You find him, Chad, and when you do, you kill him!" she screamed.

Chad took her in his arms. "I will, sis. I promise."

BOOK TWO

THE SEARCH

CHAPTER FOURTEEN

"WHAT HAVE YOU GOT, NEAL?" Chad asked.

"Whoa boy, slow down," Kade interrupted. "How are you doing?"

Chad stood still for what seemed like a lot longer than it actually was. Then he said, "I know you've been through stuff like this a lot more than me in your life. How did you get through it? I feel like I'm dying inside."

Kade said, "I know, buddy. My answer is that I didn't. I was a raving alcoholic until someone saved me, a very special someone, you. My best advice is that you just keep on keeping on. What do you say? Let's make sure Peter Strickland never hurts anyone again."

Chad took a deep breath, "Okay. But, when we do find him, I'm going to be the one who takes care of business, deal?"

"Deal."

"All right. Back to you Neal, what have you got?"

"A lot. Victor Steele has taught me a few things about hiding information and money and the deception that goes with it. There are no rules when it comes to crime."

Kade said, "I'm glad he's on our side now. I'll bet you taught him a thing or two about technology and its capabilities."

Neal smiled, "I may have enlightened him a bit. What we found out so far, Chad, is that Wainwright's import/export business was a front for the age-old sin, drugs."

"What kind?"

"Heroin. We know the *where*, but we're not clear on the *how*."

Chad said, "Where?"

Kade said, "Thailand."

"You said you don't know the entire how. What do you know?"

"It's not good. We're reasonably sure that our military is being used as the vehicle to get the drugs to Newfoundland and then from there to Wainwright's warehouse."

"You mean these drugs are getting to Canada via one of our military transports?"

Neal said, "Yes. Now we have to find out who's running the operation over there. Obviously it has to be very high up in the chain of command. How high we don't know."

Agent Brimhall had been sitting quietly so far. "Sounds like we need to go to Thailand. I'll call the Director to see if he can run some interference for us."

"Do it," Chad said, "Do it now!"

Ender looked at Kade who nodded. He took out his phone and made the call.

Kade said, "Are the newlyweds safe and sound on their honeymoon?"

"Yes, I've got them safely tucked away at a private resort. The only ones that know where they're at are those in this room and the pilot of our corporate jet. So if anything happens to them, I'll know it was one of you. I don't want to scare any of you but castration comes to mind."

"Ouch!" Kade groaned.

"Kade, before we head for Thailand, I want you to make a quick trip to Miami," Chad said.

"I agree, maybe I can track Strickland down and save us a trip."

"No. We are definitely going to Thailand. I want Peter to think he's reeling us into his web. If we already know where he is when we get there, so much the advantage for us. Plus we'll destroy his drug operation and maybe saved a few souls."

Kade said, "I'll leave tonight."

"Don't forget your persuader."

––––––

"Why do you have to go to Thailand?"

"Because Mac, we're pretty sure that if we expose the drug trafficking operation, it could destroy Strickland's cash flow and lead us to him."

"But why you? I know you're terribly upset about almost losing your grandfather, but why can't the government take over? Isn't that what the CIA does?"

"Yes they do, sweetie, and they do it very well. But with the cooperation of the FBI and CIA, Kade and I will be able to cross boundary lines of authority, cut through the red tape, and get to the truth quicker. I don't want Peter Strickland to be free any longer than necessary."

Mackenzie said, "You mean breathing any longer than necessary, don't you?"

Chad said nothing.

––––––

KADE ARRIVED in Miami a little after midnight and checked into the Hilton to catch a few hours of sleep. "Thanks, Chad," Kade whispered as he looked around the spacious suite. The next morning he had breakfast in one of the hotel's restaurants while mapping out his strategy for the day. Actually, he knew pretty much what he was going to do so he lingered over a cup of coffee and then left the hotel, turned left and began walking leisurely towards his destination. Three blocks later he smiled as he came to a building with a sign that read Brett's Tavern. He strolled in, looking like a guy who didn't have a care in the world, walked straight to the bar and sat on a stool.

"Hi, Bobby," he said to the bartender.

Bobby smiled. "I'm sorry, sir, you have me at a disadvantage. I'm usually pretty good at remembering faces. Do I know you?"

Kade said, "Yes and no. We met about six months ago, only it was my evil twin. Kade then said, in his best British accent, "Colin Lethridge. I met your good friends, Ryker and his pet monkey, Ming."

"Now I remember. You told me that you didn't think they'd be bothering me anymore, which turned out to be prophetic. Are you the one I thank for that?"

"Sorry," Kade said with a twinkle in his eye. "I haven't seen them either. Maybe the swine flu got them."

Bobby stared at Kade for a moment, then smiling said, "Right. So what do I call you now, Mr. Lethridge?"

"My friends call me Kade," he said, extending his hand.

Bobby shook Kade's hand. "Nice to meet you again, Kade. So what brings you to our establishment after six months?"

"Obviously I was working undercover at the time. We still haven't apprehended the one who runs the organization that was shaking you, and others in the area, down. We had him but he got away. My question to you is how is the collection business? Are you still getting harassed for protection money?"

"No; after you took care of Ry... er, I mean after Ryker and Ming mysteriously disappeared, I was left alone for about a month. At first people were coming around looking for them, then one day they came in demanding protection money again."

"What did you do?"

"Well at about the same time a group of cops started coming in and meeting here after work. After a few visits we hit it off and I felt like I could trust them. I explained to them what had been going on over the last few years and they told me that if anyone came in again demanding money I was to tell them. So a few days later when Jimmy came in..."

"Wait, who's Jimmy?"

"Oh sorry. Jimmy used to be one of Ryker's boys. I guess when it was determined that Ryker was not coming back, Jimmy must've been promoted. So when he came in making his demands, my new friends from the Miami Police were here. I excused myself and told the cops about it. They immediately went over to Jimmy. I don't know what they said but Jimmy left immediately. I haven't seen him since."

Kade asked, "Do you know where I can find him?"

"No, I don't, but that guy over there, sitting at that booth in the bright yellow shirt, is part of his group. He'd know."

"Thanks," Kade said. "Here's my card if you think of anything else. I'd really appreciate it." Kade paid for his drink and left Bobby a nice tip, then walked over to the table where Jimmy's associate and two others were sitting.

Kade said, "Gentlemen, I'm looking for Jimmy. I'd appreciate it if you could let me know where I can find him."

The one in the yellow shirt said, "Who wants to know?"

"Uh, I do, stupid. I thought I made that clear. Tell you what, you tell Jimmy that Kade is looking for him and it would be in his best interest to get in touch with me ASAP. Do you think you can do that or should I write it out in crayon for you?"

Kade didn't wait for an answer. He turned and headed for the door. Outside he hid behind a pillar next to the door. As predicted, the three men came barreling out the door.

They quickly looked around. "Where'd he go?"

"Behind you, boys," Kade said.

They whirled around to see Kade smiling with his Glock in his hand.

"Steady, boys; don't do anything to make this gun go off. I don't think I could stand the thought of any one of you getting hurt because of me. Now who's going to tell me where Jimmy is?"

Yellow shirt was definitely in charge. "You get nothing from us."

"I like that, loyal to a fault. Let's go for a walk. There's an alley next to the building."

They hesitated so Kade motioned with his gun towards the alley. They began walking, Kade following. He looked at yellow shirt, "Give me your phone."

"Why?"

"Sorry boy, but I ask the questions." Kade then raised his gun to where the man could see it was pointing at his forehead. He reached into his pocket and pulled out his phone.

"Thank you. That didn't hurt now did it?" He then motioned for the three men to move up against the far wall, about ten feet from where Kade stood. He took the phone and held it in front of his face so that he could look at it while still keeping his eyes on the three men across from him. "Now let's see, I could start dialing phone numbers in here and if I do finally get Jimmy, I don't think he'll be too happy with your circumstances, do you? By the way, what is your name?" he asked yellow shirt.

"The name is Art, and you're going to remember it very well when I'm through with you!"

"Okay, Art. Do I make the call or do you?"

Art pondered the question and decided he'd better do it. "Give me the phone," he snapped.

Kade said nothing as he handed him back his phone. Art pushed a number on speed dial.

"This better be important," the voice on the other end said.

"Jimmy, we've got a situation here."

Kade grabbed the phone back. "Jimmy, listen up. I have three of your boys here. If you ever want to see them again, I'd suggest you meet me at the Motel 6 on Jeffrey Avenue in one hour."

"Who is this?"

"Someone who has your best interest at heart. I also have some information about Ryker and Ming that I think you'll be interested in. If you come alone you and your boys will not be harmed. If you don't come alone, I assure you I have the manpower and capabilities of inflicting heavy punishment on you and them. Don't be late. Room 106." Kade hit the end button and put the phone in his pocket. "You boys have been so good. I just need to make one more call. Sit down on the ground, would you please?" Kade had a silencer on his gun so when they didn't respond to his request he fired a shot in between the feet of two of them. They quickly sat down.

"That's better," Kade said. "Almost done." He then called Ender on his phone, explained the situation, giving his location, and asked him to send a couple of the local FBI guys to pick the three men up and put them somewhere where they couldn't make any phone calls for a week or two.

When he was finished he smiled at them. "What do you think? Do the Heat have a chance without LeBron? I think maybe they'll get to the playoffs, but that's it."

———

THIRTY MINUTES LATER, the boys from the FBI picked Art and his cronies up. Kade made his way to the motel to get things ready for Jimmy. Thirty-five minutes later there was a knock at the door. Kade slowly opened the door. A man thirty something, slightly overweight and balding, was standing alone. "You must be Jimmy. You know you're five minutes late, but that's okay. Come on in." Kade had his gun hidden behind his back. As soon as Jimmy was inside Kade brought out the gun, as Jimmy was about to do the same thing. "I wouldn't if I were you. Put the gun down slowly on the floor and sit in the chair over there."

Jimmy sat down. While Kade was tying Jimmy's hands behind his back, Jimmy asked, "Who are you? Do you have any idea who you are messing with or what we are capable of doing to you?"

"You know, that's exactly what Ryker told me. After I put a bullet in Ming's forehead, Ryker and I had a nice visit. Well, maybe for me, not so nice for Ryker. I guess you never saw him cry like a baby, did you? He finally gave me the info I needed, as you will. It just depends on how you want to do this."

Kade walked to the tray that was sitting near the chair, opened up his kit, and spread out the instruments. "What's that?" Jimmy asked nervously.

"I call it the persuader, Jimmy. Ryker didn't like it very much. Now, here's the thing. Ryker didn't make it, but you on the other hand, can. You'll walk out of here unscathed if you give me the right answers."

"You're bluffing," Jimmy scoffed.

"Wrong first answer. One more and we begin. Now, let me tell you what I already know and then what you are going to tell me. First of all, I know you are small potatoes in Peter Strickland's organization."

Jimmy's head snapped up. "You're with Chad Hamilton." He grinned. "You *are* a dead man and don't know it."

"There you go again, quoting Ryker. Ming said the same thing too, one second before he died." Jimmy's smile immediately turned to a frown. "As you already know, Chad and I brought Peter down. Now you know we also took out Ming and Ryker, and the assassin, Carter, whom Chad killed. I'm not lying; you can walk or you can suffer the kind of pain that you never knew existed. All I want from you is the whereabouts of Peter Strickland. It's that simple. What's it going to be?"

Jimmy said nothing.

"Oh good, I haven't been able to do this since Ryker." He started picking up different instruments. The first looked like some kind of surgical blade. "I like this one. The blade is so sharp I can remove all your fingernails in a matter of seconds" He lowered the blade, setting it back on the table. Then he picked up what looked like a pair of pliers. "This is my favorite. I call it the nutcracker. Hmm...maybe I'll save it for later."

As Kade was setting it down the door burst open. Two guys entered with their guns drawn. "Freeze! Get your hands up!"

Jimmy said, "What took you so long? Untie me then get him into this chair and tie him up." Once Kade was secured in the chair, Jimmy said, "Not so bad now, are you tough guy?"

Kade said, "Bad enough to handle you ladies."

Jimmy smiled and then hit Kade in the mouth, snapping his head back and drawing blood from his lip. "You two soften him up while I check out these tools." One of the thugs began pounding on Kade with brutal blows to his body and face.

He stopped for a second and Kade said, "Is that all you got?"

The other guy stepped in, hitting Kade in the face. The left side was starting to bruise, his lower lip was swollen, and the right side of his face was smeared with blood dripping from the gash above his right eye. He started to strike him again when Jimmy ordered him to stop.

"You gentlemen leave me something to work with. I want him awake the whole time. You can have him when I'm done, although I doubt if there will be anything left."

Kade said, "You know Jimmy I was trying to do the right thing and let you walk after we had our little chat, but now I've changed my mind."

"Still talking tough, are we big guy? I never did get your name."

"My friends call me Kade. You can call me sir."

Jimmy laughed as he shook his head. "I'll give you one thing, Kade, you've got balls." Then he looked at the instruments. "That gives me an idea. Why don't we start with, what did you call it, the nutcracker?"

"It takes a little intelligence to use that and since you obviously don't have any of that, I'd suggest you use something a little less complicated."

Jimmy said, "Oh, I'm going to enjoy this." He fiddled with the instrument and said, "How do you open these?"

Kade said, "You don't really think I'm going to tell you, do you, stupid?"

"A sense of humor to the end, huh, tough guy? I like that. It's going to make this all the better to hear your screams." He noticed the knob at the bottom of one of the handles. "Ah, here we go." He twisted the knob to release both handles when it exploded in his face.

CHAPTER FIFTEEN

STILL TIED TO THE CHAIR, Kade sprang to his feet and kicked one of the guys in the groin. He immediately fell to his knees, howling in agony. Jimmy was already yelling with his hands in his face. That left one guy to be dealt with. Kade maneuvered over to the tray holding the surgical instruments and started groping behind his back. He grabbed something sharp and began cutting at the rope. The third guy had recovered from the shock of what happened and pounced on Kade just as he cut through the rope. His arms and hands were now free but the third guy was on top of him with the second guy was getting up to help. Fortunately, Jimmy was still writhing in pain and blinded by the explosion. But the other two were in full frontal attack and obviously at the advantage because of Kade's weakened condition. They had him pinned down on the floor when Jimmy yelled, "Forget keeping him alive. Shoot him!"

"I don't think so," came the voice by the door. Because Jimmy's men had broken the handle on the door, the door was easily opened. Standing inside the frame of the door were the two FBI agents who had arrested the men in the alley, ninety minutes earlier. With their guns pointing at them, the two guys that had Kade pinned, stood up, raising their hands in the air. Jimmy was still in pain.

"Nice to see you guys," Kade said. "I was just getting on top of them when you arrived."

"Right," Agent Barret chuckled. "I could see that."

Kade got to his feet and set the chair upright while the agents cuffed the two men. He walked over to Jimmy, grabbed him and sat him down. He then went into the bathroom, got a towel and wet it. He gave it to Jimmy. "Wipe your eyes, dirt bag. That explosive was mostly pepper and chili powder. You'll be okay in a few."

Agent Barret said, "Are we done here?"

"Yeah, thanks boys. Take them and secure them with the others. I'll be along shortly."

Jimmy looked confused. "Wait a minute. I know my rights. Me and my friends want to call our lawyer."

"Sorry, Jimmy, but when you hooked up with a sleazeball like Peter Strickland, you gave up your rights." The agents smiled at Kade, turned and left with Jimmy's boys.

"You can't do this!"

"Oh, but I can, and will. Now be a good boy and give me your phone."

Jimmy stared at Kade a few seconds, then reached into his pocket and handed over his phone.

"So, Jimmy, which of these numbers will lead me to Peter Strickland. Hmm... here's an interesting prefix. I wonder where that will lead me." After some persuasive threats with his kit, but not actually using it, Kade got the info he was after.

"Okay, Jimmy, we're done here. Remember when I told you I wasn't going to let you go, after you and your boys were so rude to me?"

Jimmy said nothing.

"Well, I lied." Kade walked over to the door, opened it and motioned for Agent Barret and his partner.

As Jimmy was being led away Kade said, "Once you boys are

released in a couple of weeks, I'd suggest you disappear permanently, because the Peter Strickland I know will never let you live. Trust me on this or it will be the last thing you do in this life."

———

An hour later Kade called Chad. "I think we got a partial location on Strickland."

Chad said, "Great. Where is he?"

"Rio De Janeiro, Brazil. I don't know that for sure, but when I mentioned it to Peter's goon Jimmy, the look on his face gave him away. So what do you say, Chad? Shall we go straight to Rio and find Peter and end this?"

"No, as much as I'd like to, we go to Thailand first, destroy his drug operation and let him think he's bringing us in. We leave in two days. We're going to meet with a General Chambers at the Army base near Bangkok. Ender says the General is a boyhood friend of his boss, Ken Stout, and can be trusted. He'll run interference for us."

"Okay. I'll see you tomorrow. I'm flying out tonight. Maybe we can meet with Neal and Ender before we leave."

"Already got it set up for ten in the morning."

"Why am I not surprised?"

———

"I don't understand. Why do you have to go to Thailand?"

"I told you, Mac. This is part of an FBI investigation that I happen to be responsible for. And now that we're going to Thailand and eventually Rio, the CIA is also going to help. Peter Strickland has to be brought down, operation and all. Our family will never be safe until then. I think you know that."

Mackenzie sighed, "I know. You just promise me, my knight in shining armor, that you'll be careful and come back to me safe and sound."

"I promise." Chad tenderly kissed her. "How would you like to come to Rio when the time comes?"

"Seriously? I'd love it. I'm surprised you're even considering it."

"Kade and I discussed it last night. It will be strictly on the QT. Not a word to anyone about it except Sydney. Kade says she's got lots of vacation time coming and intends to use it. The way we look at it, you two lethal weapons can protect us better than any trained experts. Anyway, we'll see. Kade and I are going to evaluate it further in Thailand. We figure it would be too lonely without you two nagging at us."

Mackenzie narrowed her eyes.

"I'm not making any promises, but Kade is working on a couple of passports for both of you. We'll bring you in separately so that Peter and his people won't know. That's the only way I'll allow it."

"Then you better well, come back to me. And I think you know why."

Chad smiled, "I think I do."

"Yep, I've never been to Rio."

————

"WHAT HAVE WE GOT SO FAR?" Chad asked

Kade said, "We arrive tomorrow night at Bangkok's Suvarnab-humi Airport. Since we're taking the corporate jet, it will fuel up and depart within forty-five minutes. No one should notice. We'll be met by Bo Davies. Bo is a CIA operative and has been briefed on our mission."

"Do you know him?" Chad asked.

"No, but he comes highly recommended. He has legendary expertise in covert operations and can go unnoticed in just about any situation."

"That sounds good. Neal, are you all set up and ready to go?"

"Ready to go as you instructed. I'll be able to do anything you want from right here in your office."

"Great. So, Ender, what do you think? Are we prepared for this?"

"As prepared as we can be. There will be twists and turns along the way. There always are. I don't know about you guys, but I'm excited."

"Me too," Kade said. "The adrenaline is really flowing."

"All right then. Let's relax for a few hours and then get this thing done."

———

KADE WAS SITTING next to Sydney on her couch with the TV going. They were watching a previously recorded episode of Doctor Who. "So are you two nutcases really going to let Mackenzie and me join you in Rio?"

"As long as we can keep it completely secret. There's no way Chad is going to put you two in harm's way."

"What about you, Michael?" Kade's full name was Jacob Michael Kincaid. Ever since Sydney learned that, she said she was going to call him Michael. He liked it!

"Personally, I pity the poor fool who messes with you two. When we find Strickland, I'm going to suggest to Chad that we sic you ladies on him."

Sydney said, "I like your thinking. I'd like a piece of that guy."

"He'd definitely regret it. Seriously though, I hope we can wrap up this drug thing in Thailand quickly. Then off to Rio to nail Strickland and then the four of us can have some much needed R & R."

"Do you think it can go that smoothly?"

"It never goes the way it's planned but hopefully Chad and I are prepared for anything that gets in the way."

"Or who," Sydney groaned.

Kade's phone rang. "Hold on, Syd, this might be important." He held his hand up to pause Sydney. "Hey, sweetie, how are you?"

"Sweetie?"

"Okay, it's Chad. Were you jealous for just a second?" Kade teased.

"Jealous is not the word I was thinking of, you..."

"What's up, Cupcake? Wasn't two hours with me this morning enough?"

"Two hours was way too much for your ugly puss. Would you like some good news?"

"I'm getting a raise?!"

Chad snickered. "Are you kidding? I just saw your last month's expense report. I think you owe me. But, I digress. The trip to Thailand is off."

CHAPTER SIXTEEN

"How come? Did you miss last month's payment on your little Gulfstream?"

"Something like that. Meeting tomorrow at 9:00 a.m. sharp, or in your case, sometime before 9:30. However, the coffee and donuts will be gone by 9:15."

"Are you bringing my favorite?"

"Yes, your bear claws will be there. Bring Sydney if she can get away. We could use her input. I've also invited Victor. We can use an ex-liar and cheat on this one."

Kade said, "Well, he is the best. See you in the morning."

As Kade hung up, Sydney said, "What was that all about?"

"I'm not sure, but the trip to Thailand is off."

"Permanently?"

"Not sure of that either. Chad didn't seem to be too concerned. Actually he was in a rather good mood."

"Why do you call him Cupcake?"

"You haven't heard that story? I thought everyone knew by now."

Sydney shook her head.

"When Chad joined the Army he was an emotional wreck. But

his superiors didn't notice. All they knew was that this kid had special skills."

"What kind of skills?"

"First of all, at 6′1″ and a body that looked like it had been chiseled out of stone..."

"It still does," Sydney interrupted.

"Whoa there, missy. I thought you said you only had eyes for me?"

"I do, but you are always standing next to him. A girl can look, can't she? If it makes you feel any better, it looks like the same artist sculpted both your bodies."

"Good answer, Syd. Now where was I? Oh yeah, as I said, he was not only big but had cat-like speed and hand-to-hand skills that were unparalleled. And his leadership evaluations were off the charts. It was a surprise to no one when he was promoted to lieutenant and put in charge of his own Special Forces unit. Because he was so green and had literally no knowledge of the small African country we were in, I was assigned by a joint decision from the Army and the CIA, particularly your dad, to be a part of his unit as an advisor."

"Are we getting to the Cupcake part yet?" Sydney joked. "I'm hungry."

"What Cupcake part? Who's Cupcake?"

"All right, smart boy. I'm all ears."

"Your ears are not what I'm interested in," Kade teased. "Although that's always a good starting point." He gave her a wicked smile.

"Get to the point!" Sydney shouted trying to contain her laughter.

"Okay, okay. So Chad's reason for joining the Army was because of the death of his girlfriend, Jenny. He completely flipped out. It was six months before his family and friends even knew where he was."

"I remember hearing this from Katie."

"Right, so anyway, Chad came into this assignment with a major attitude problem, almost suicidal. Our missions were dangerous enough without having a leader who took unnecessary chances, *really* unnecessary ones. Well, as their leader, nobody in his squadron could stand up to him or especially call him names that were, shall we say, extremely not Christian."

Sydney said, "I think I'm starting to get the picture."

"Yes, well, I wasn't under that same set of rules, so I started calling him Cupcake, mostly to his back but sometimes face to face."

"I'll bet he was thrilled."

"Oh yeah. After our second or third mission you could see a change beginning to take place. I think he was starting to realize that life as he thought he knew it, wasn't so bad compared to what these people we were trying to help were going through just to survive. But he most definitely was irritated by the Cupcake handle I'd given him. Actually it's what I was trying to do, irritate him. He was just the opposite of that term."

"So...."

"So anyway, he pulled me aside one day, or should I say, jerked me aside, and confronted me. We were literally nose to nose. If the truth be told, we about came to blows right then and there. But my charm came through."

"Oh brother, your modesty doth make you charismatic."

"Why thank you, missy. Actually Lieutenant Hamilton cursed my ancestry and threatened to place my rifle where the sun don't shine if I didn't quit calling him Cupcake and show him a little respect in front of his men. So I came right back at him and told him his recklessness was going to get one or all of us killed. I also told him his men didn't respect him and that sooner or later, probably sooner, he was going to get a bullet in the back of his head if he didn't start looking out for the safety of his men."

"I'll bet he wasn't too thrilled about that."

"No he wasn't. He started to bark something back at me but thought otherwise and went silent. After a minute he moved to the nearest tree, sat down, and buried his head in his hands."

"What did you do?"

"Chad looked so helpless and pathetic, I sat down next to him, put my arm around him, and then we kissed."

Sydney said, "You know, sometimes I really hate you!"

Kade put his arms around Sydney. "No you don't; you love me and you know it."

Sydney tried to suppress a smile. "There's that Kincaid modesty again."

"Hard to resist, isn't it?"

"So tell me please, what really happened after you sat down with Chad?"

"Nothing for a minute or two. Then he opened up and told me all about Jenny and how, after she died, he hated God, hated himself, and just plain hated life. He couldn't remember joining the army or his rapid rise to a lieutenant in charge of a Special Forces unit. He talked about his present feelings after our first few weeks in the field and how life, as he knew it, wasn't so awful compared to what these people were going through every day of theirs. Anyway, when we were through, he apologized and the beginning of a great friendship ensued."

"What about the Cupcake tag?"

"Oh, well, when he got up to apologize he stuck out his hand. I reciprocated and said, 'It's okay, Cupcake, we're good.' I figured he'd either laugh to relieve the tension or shoot me dead right on the spot."

"So..."

"I'm here, aren't I?"

Sydney put her arms up around Kade's neck and gave him a long lingering kiss. "Yes, you are. I think I'll keep you."

———

KADE ARRIVED at Chad's penthouse at exactly 9:00 a.m. sharp, Sydney on his arm, and went straight for the donut box. He picked out a bear claw. "Ah, it's the little things in life."

Chad walked over and hugged Sydney. "Glad you could make it,

Syd. You and the bear claw are the only reason he's here on time. Better grab a donut before he devours them all."

Kade said nothing, as his mouth was so full that he could barely breathe. Everyone in the room had a good laugh. Already sitting were Ender, Neal, and Victor. As Kade and Sydney were settling in on an adjoining sofa, Chad got things rolling. "Okay, let's get started."

Kade said, "So the trip is off?"

"No," Chad said. "The trip to Thailand is off. We're going to South Korea."

CHAPTER SEVENTEEN

Kade said, "And the reason is?"

"Neal and I think Peter Strickland is throwing us a curve, a little diversion. Putting it mildly, he's playing with us. Tell me, Kade, besides being a sleazeball, what else do we know about him?"

"Well, as far as criminals go, he's brilliant."

Chad said, "Exactly. He was a major player in the drug world in Miami for over 20 years, and here in Boston he was the golden boy, admired by everyone. You don't do that without brains. Now let's go back to the day we found Wainwright's body. What did we find?"

"Nothing," Kade said. "Except for his cell phone. That was the break we needed."

Chad said, "Was it?"

Kade paused. "He set us up, didn't he?"

"I think so. That phone is what led us to Thailand. The base we were headed for is no more than a small group of buildings that house the soldiers who guard the Embassy. Nothing more. So yesterday after you all left, Neal went back to the location in Newfoundland and worked backwards. Come to find out, we think that the Hovey Army Base in Seoul is where the drugs came from.

Ender is working on setting us up over there. In the meantime we're going to assume that Peter has eyes on us so we are going to proceed as if we are going to Thailand as planned. The corporate jet is going to take us to the airport in Bangkok. That's what the official flight plan shows. The plan then shows the jet returning to Logan airport in Boston."

Kade said, "Won't they have someone watching us get off the plane and proceeding to the hotel?"

"And that's exactly what they'll see. Hours before we get on the plane, three guys that the FBI is providing will get on the plane. They will have the same height and build as you, Ender, and me. Then we will all fly to Thailand. They will get off, which is what the bad guys will see. We will then take off for Seoul. The official flight plan will show the jet going to Logan thanks to our friends at the CIA."

"How long do you think it will take Strickland to realize it's not us in Thailand?" Kade asked.

Ender said. "Maybe he won't. These guys from the FBI are used to doing covert stuff like this. Strickland is the only one who knows what we look like up close. If and when it's figured out what we've done, we should be finished in Korea."

"I like your optimism. And if things go wrong, we've got our boy to make everything come out alright."

Chad sighed. "Thanks for the vote of confidence. Hopefully everything will go as planned, although it never does, does it?"

"No it doesn't." Kade said. "That's where the fun comes in."

"As long as someone doesn't get hurt, or worse," Ender added.

"We leave tomorrow morning, so go out and party, get some rest, and do whatever you want. Kade and I are taking the ladies out to dinner. See you bright and early."

———

"I'M GOING to have the Pork Salad," Chad said.

Kade raised an eyebrow. "That doesn't sound very Mexican to

me." Chad and Kade were dining with Mackenzie and Sydney at Juan's Mexican Restaurant in the Hamilton Towers.

Mackenzie said, "Trust me, Kade, it's to die for. Juan's spicy green sauce is great and has a pretty good kick to it. I think I'm going with my favorite, Juan's Special Burrito Supreme, enchilada style."

"That sounds good," Sydney said. "Make that two Specials."

"You people have no adventure in you." Kade looked at the waiter. "I'll have the Atomic Bomb." It was listed on the menu as a quesadilla with three cheeses and Juan's secret habanero sauce (not for the faint of heart).

"It's your funeral," Chad said. "I had a little taste of Juan's secret sauce and it nearly burned my tongue off. Don't forget we have an early flight in the morning."

"Ah, it couldn't be any worse than those spicy chicken wings we had in Taiwan three years ago."

"No, you're right about that," Chad said. "I couldn't feel my face for hours."

Kade smiled at Sydney. "You should have seen him Syd. Ol' Chad's not much of a drinker but he was in so much pain that, after a few drinks, I'm not sure if he was numb from the pain or the alcohol."

Mackenzie sighed, "I think I learn more about you at these dinners we have together than anywhere else, Chad. Are there any more secrets I need to know before you make an honest woman out of me?"

Sydney jerked forward in her chair. "What! Are you saying...?"

Chad's face turned bright red as Mackenzie said. "We haven't made any formal plans or announcements but, yes, Chad lowered his guard a couple of weeks ago and I jumped all over it. He's mine forever and I'm not about to let him off the hook."

"No worries, Mac. It's the best decision I've ever made. Once we get this Peter Strickland mess over with, we will be making some serious plans."

Kade said, "That's awesome. Hey what about getting married at home plate on opening day next year?"

Sydney groaned. "That's my man, so romantic."

"What?" Kade asked innocently.

"Don't you know what every girl dreams of?" Chad asked.

"I suppose so. Anyway, congrats."

"Thanks, big guy. You know, I'll be needing a best man." Kade suppressed a smile as Chad said. "I was thinking of my grandpa; whaddya think?"

Kade tried to hide his disappointment. "I think your grandpa would be honored and..."

"Gotcha!" Chad laughed. "Did you see the look on his sour puss, ladies? Priceless. I don't know what kind of a wedding Mackenzie will plan, and it's entirely up to her, but you're my best man. You just make sure you wear clean underwear and take a bath."

Kade came right back. "On the same day!? I sure hope it's a Saturday."

"I'll make sure he's not only presentable," Sydney said, "but maybe next to Chad only, he'll be the handsomest guy there."

Chad said, "Good luck with that, Syd."

———

The flight from Boston to Suvarnabhumi Airport in Bangkok, Thailand took sixteen hours. When it arrived the three agents disembarked as planned, while Chad, Kade, and Ender watched. The fuel truck filled the Gulfstream's tanks and after approximately forty minutes, they took off for Seoul, South Korea.

"I sure hope this works," Ender said.

"It'll work," Chad said. "First thing tomorrow morning, we have a meeting with the commanding officer, General Markum. Then we'll do a little snooping around to get the lay of the land."

"Sounds good. What about Sunday? Not much going on at the base," Kade said. "Maybe a little sightseeing in Seoul?"

"Way ahead of you, big guy," Chad said.

"Why am I not surprised? What exactly do you have in mind for us?"

"Baseball."

"Baseball! In Korea? Are you kidding me?"

Chad laughed. "Baseball is huge there."

Kade looked at Ender. "Can you believe this guy, baseball?"

"Works for me. We could use a little R & R after almost twenty-four hours of flying."

Kade said, "Okay, Chad. I suppose you have something in mind besides just the pure enjoyment of watching a game."

"Yep, there's a pitcher from the visiting team, the Samsung Lions out of Daegu, that's terrific."

"What's his name, Lon Jon Poop?" Kade said sarcastically.

"Not funny, man. His name is Mun Hui-Su."

"Isn't that what I just said?"

"Not even close," Chad laughed. "I'll have to line up an interpreter in order to talk to him. I'd like to get to him before the other teams even know about him."

"How do you know about him?" asked Ender.

"When I told Treat we were headed for Seoul, he spent all night researching the South Korean baseball league. Right now, Hui-Su is under the radar but seems to be loaded with amazing potential. He's 6'2" and has a fastball that's been clocked at 100 miles an hour."

"SHUT UP!"

Chad laughed. "That's what Treat and I want to find out. He could be a diamond in the rough."

"Sounds like fun. Do you think they have hot dogs at these games?"

Chad said, "It would be un-American if they didn't."

"Exactly." quipped Kade.

———

AFTER A TWO-HOUR FLIGHT, the plane descended and eventually

landed at Incheon International Airport in Seoul. As our heroes departed the Hamilton Jet, an Army officer was waiting for them with a standard unmarked sedan. He introduced himself as Lieutenant Bowers and indicated that General Markum had ordered him to pick them up and escort them to the base. They were immediately escorted into the General's office, which was rather small and unremarkable. Markum got up quickly, extending his hand. He looked intimidating, standing at 6'6" with graying short-cropped hair. At age 58, he had definitely seen better days physically, sporting a rather imposing stomach which intimated that he had spent a lot of time at his desk the last few years. This was going to be his last assignment before retirement. "Robert Markum."

Chad introduced his team and then said, "Thanks for allowing us to come and stir up some trouble, General."

General Markum said, "I've been in this man's army for nearly 35 years, so there's not much that catches me off-guard. But I am a little surprised by what you're saying, and if it's true, very pissed off. Are you sure that we've got a drug distribution operation going on here right under my nose?"

"No, General, we're not. That's why we're here. But all indications say that there is. We are dealing with a master criminal with a brilliant mind and the resources to pull off even the most intricate operations without being detected." Chad then gave Markum the details of all that they knew about Peter Strickland.

Markum said, "This guy sounds like a genius with absolutely no conscience. Not a great combination for the good guys."

"You're right about that," Chad said. "But we are going to get Paul Stevens, aka Peter Strickland, and it starts here."

General Markum came up out of his chair, "Did you say Paul Stevens?"

CHAPTER EIGHTEEN

ENDER SAID, "YOU KNOW HIM!?"

"I don't know him personally but I know *of* him. I've been here for a little over four years and anything drug related or illegal has his signature on it. I thought we had finally gotten rid of his influence around here and now you're telling me he's behind this new supposed operation?"

"No *supposed* about it, General," Chad said. "We don't know a lot yet but we do know that whatever is happening, Paul Stevens has to be involved."

General Markum shook his head. "I really thought you guys were here on a wild goose chase, but now, Paul Stevens. I can't believe it."

Kade said, "Believe it, General. This guy is as good as it gets."

"Our biggest challenge here," Chad said, "is we don't know how he's getting the drugs out of here. We have good reason to believe that they are coming from here, but no clue as to how."

"How can I help?"

"If you could provide us a list of your supply line, those that start all shipping orders down to the person who actually fills them, I'd appreciate it. Since it's Saturday night, we'll start first thing Monday morning. Tomorrow we'll browse around and get the lay of the land."

Ender said, "You mean take in a ball game."

"You boys like baseball?" General Markum said.

Kade and Ender looked at Chad and smiled. Then Kade proceeded to share with the General Chad's involvement in major league baseball.

"My, my," General Markum said. "What's a businessman like you doing here on this operation with the CIA and the FBI?"

"Actually, General," Ender said. "Chad's in charge."

The General looked somewhat confused. He studied Chad for a moment. "Who are you?"

"Just a concerned citizen, sir, accepting a request from an official up the chain of command."

"Actually," Kade said. "Chad's the first in over 2000 years to walk on water, isn't that right, Cupcake?"

Chad threw a disgusted look in Kade's direction, stood up and extended his hand to Markum. "Thanks for your help. I hope we can bring this problem to a quick solution. Care to catch a ballgame with us tomorrow?"

"Thanks, but no. But I'll bet my assistant, Lieutenant Bowers, might take you up on it. He's a big fan of the Seoul Doosan Bears. They'll be facing your super pitcher tomorrow."

The General called Lieutenant Bowers into his office and Chad extended the invitation, which Bowers enthusiastically accepted.

———

"YOU'RE RIGHT, CHAD," Kade said. "These hot dogs are as good as any I've ever had. They always taste better at a ballgame."

"I readily concur," Ender said.

"Readily concur!" Kade teased. "This is a baseball game, not a literature class. Knock off those big words so Chad can understand."

Chad looked over to Lieutenant Bowers. "Never a dull moment with these two. Are you enjoying yourself?"

"I'm having a great time, thanks. Although it would be a lot better if that pitcher you're interested in would allow my Bears a hit or two."

"I know, he's terrific, isn't he? Do you speak Korean?"

"I get by."

"Maybe we can talk to Hui-Su after the game." Chad turned to Kade and Ender. "You two notice the uniforms over there scoping us out?"

Ender said, "Yeah, and also the guys over there in the suits."

"I thought this mission was supposed to be top secret?" Chad said.

"Not to worry, boys, we get that all the time. It's most likely because you're with me. Even though we have excellent relations with the South Koreans, we are still foreigners and not on their most loved list."

"Good to know," Chad said. "But we're still going to keep an eye on them."

———

IMMEDIATELY FOLLOWING THE GAME, the boys worked their way down to the clubhouse. With Lieutenant Bowers leading the way they were able to get an audience with the manager of the Samsung Lions and his star pitcher Mun Hui-Su. With Bowers doing an adequate job of translation, Chad was able to tell Hui-Su who exactly he was and his interest in possibly bringing him to Major League Baseball in North America, and particularly to Montreal. He asked if he could continue corresponding with Hui-Su and keep both sides apprised of their situation. He also gave Hui-Su's manager his card so that they could keep in touch as well. After their brief meeting, Bowers showed the boys around Seoul to finish off their afternoon, then Chad took them to dinner at one of Seoul's finest restaurants. They had Bowers order their food.

"This tastes great!" Kade said. "What is it? Never mind, I don't want to know. Could be some cow's bowel or something. Ruin everything. I'll just enjoy it."

Chad said, "Good idea, Kade. It really is delicious. I'll bet it kills the food at the base, doesn't it, Lieutenant?"

"That it does. But I think you'll be pleasantly surprised at our cuisine."

"I'll take your word for it," Chad said with a touch of skepticism. "So, Lieutenant, what do you think of our theory that there is a big drug operation going on right under your noses?"

"To be honest with you Chad, nothing surprises me anymore. Things are pretty sloppy around here lately."

"How so?"

"As you know all too well, the Army is very tight and highly organized. Not so with this base. Putting it bluntly, it starts and ends with the General. This is his last stop before retirement and he seems to be a little burned out. He's definitely not running a tight ship, or in this case, base."

"Do you think it might be the reason for the drug dealing that's going on?" Ender asked.

"It could be, if there really is a problem. I don't want to offend you boys but I'm not convinced yet that there is a problem. It's going to be a real embarrassment to me if there is one."

"How so?" Chad asked.

"Because, as the General's assistant, I'm supposed to know everything that's going on here. I'll cooperate any way I can if you promise me one thing."

"What's that?"

"That I get five minutes alone with whoever's behind this."

Kade laughed. "After talking with your General you may have to stand in line."

———

He didn't see any movement anywhere. It was after midnight so the base was shut down tight for the night. Getting to Hamilton was going to be a piece of cake. *I'll teach this fool a lesson he'll never forget. These three pansies won't know what hit them.* He'd received information as to Chad and his team's whereabouts and then the exact location of their private barracks. *Like shootin' ducks in a pond!* He crept closer and stationed himself next to the window and glanced inside. The next moment didn't go as planned as he felt the muzzle of the gun pressed against his temple.

Chad spoke, as he felt inside the guy's jacket, reaching for his revolver, "No sudden moves. And if you think you're good enough or fast enough to overpower me, then my friend behind you will shoot, isn't that right, Kade?"

"Right you are, my good man."

The stranger looked defeated but not alarmed. "Okay, okay, you got me. Why don't we go inside?"

"My thoughts exactly," Chad said.

The stranger was led carefully inside the barracks where Ender was sitting on a chair next to a table, revolver in hand. "Well, well," he said. "Look what we've got."

Once they were all inside where the light was good, Kade said. "Bo Davies. I can't believe it."

"How ya doin', Kade?"

"Not *the* Bo Davies?" Chad said. "You're supposed to be in Thailand."

"I was, but your FBI boys were made yesterday morning. So the Director thought it would be wise if I hightailed it over here to see if I could be of service."

"That was good of him," Kade said. "Might've been better if you had just knocked on the door."

"I wanted to see if you boys were as good as your reputation. I guess you'll do," he said, smiling.

"Thanks," Ender said. "So, Strickland knows we're not in Bangkok. What now, Chad?"

"Not a problem. We knew we'd eventually be found out. It wouldn't surprise me if Peter knows we are here in Seoul. Right now he and I are playing a game of cat and mouse. We both know what each other is about. And we both know that eventually he and I will face each other at the end. It's just a matter of time."

"Then why don't we just get our butts on over to Rio and end this?" Kade asked.

"Because the more damage we can do to his operations, the more it will piss him off. And that hopefully will lead to him making a major mistake. Advantage us. Peter hasn't lost the bulk of his income, even though we did a little damage in that area, but we destroyed his good name and reputation. He can never get that back."

Ender said, "You mean you destroyed all that. He'll never be satisfied until he destroys you and anything or anyone connected to you."

"True, I may not be on his best friend list, but that helps me in a way."

"Oh, I can't wait to hear your logic on that," Kade said.

"Strickland wants me to suffer and then confront me face to face. So technically I'm safe until then. That's why we've got my family back home under close protection and security. Oh and by the way, that means you, my friends. Better watch your backs. He only wants me to be at the finish, and maybe Kade too." Chad glanced at Kade. "You weren't very nice to him, either."

Kade grinned. "And I'm looking forward to making the last part of his life miserable before I let you finish him."

Chad yawned. "I think we should try and get a few winks in and then tomorrow we'll see what we can find out about Peter's little drug business. We'll fill you in in the morning, Bo."

―――――

ARMY LIFE STARTS EARLY in the morning and it was no exception for Chad and his team. Sitting in the mess hall with a few hundred soldiers, they sat silently eating their breakfast.

"Where do we begin?" Ender asked.

"This is where I say 'at the beginning,'" Chad answered, "wherever that is. Only the general and his assistant know why we are here. The rest of the base thinks we are an independent civilian team doing an audit of the base and its entire operation. It's supposedly authorized by some congressmen to satisfy their contingency that the armed forces are operating at full efficiency."

Kade said, "Good luck with that."

"Why, Mister Kincaid, do I detect a little sarcasm in your voice?" Ender joked.

"Not a little; just Uncle Sam at his usual best, spending the taxpayer's money."

"Only in this case, my money," Chad groaned. "That was the deal with the Director so nothing could be traced back to the FBI. Anyway, back to the business at hand. Let's start with what we know."

"We know that drugs are coming from this base, proceeding to the base in Newfoundland, and then into the States," Ender said. "So we know the *what*, but as far as this base goes, we don't know the *how* or the *who*."

"That's not entirely true."

All eyes turned to Chad. "The *who* is most likely one of four people: Lieutenant Robert White, the officer responsible for the overall operation; then there's Sergeant John Miller, who directs all supplies going in and out of the base; after that there's Corporal Leonard Thompson, Sergeant Miller's right-hand man. He is the most hands-on of the supply line. There are probably others who help along the way, but answers to one of these three."

Kade said, "You said there were four possibilities."

"The fourth would be a long shot but still should be on the list."

"Who?" Ender asked.

"General Markum's assistant, Lieutenant Bowers."

"Really?" Ender asked. "I got a good feeling about him at the ball game."

"Me too, Ender, but as you know, in your line of work, everyone is a suspect until proven innocent. So we keep an eye on Bowers too."

CIA agent Bo Davies asked, "What can I do to help?"

Kade said, "You, my friend, can do what you do best."

"What's that?"

"Watch our backs."

"No problem. It will be my pleasure. I'll even keep an eye on the FBI guy."

"Gee thanks," Ender smiled sarcastically.

Chad started to rise. "Okay, boys, let's do it."

CHAPTER NINETEEN

MACKENZIE AND SYDNEY were on their way to Hamilton Industries. The traffic was slow because of the morning congestion. "I hope we can get Katie away from work later. We need to have some fun while the guys are gone," Sydney said.

"Me too, Syd. Even though there is danger involved, you know they're having a great time."

"That I do, especially the danger part. We are probably more worried than they are."

"Right you are about that. I say we kidnap Katie and go clubbing tonight."

Sydney said, "Why, you little she devil. I think that is a great idea."

By this time they were pulling into the parking lot. "What about our friends?" Mackenzie asked, looking in the direction of the two bodyguards that were assigned to protect the ladies.

"Let's deal with them later. Right now let's see what we can do to pull Katie away from her work." They strolled into the lobby of Hamilton Industries and, as luck would have it, Katie was standing in front of them, escorting someone out that she had been in a meeting with. Her eyes caught Sydney and Mackenzie. She nearly screamed with delight as she walked quickly over and hugged them both.

Mackenzie said, "Is that any way for the CEO of a major corporation to act?"

Katie laughed. "No one can fire me, I'm the boss! Come on in. Jackie, please hold all my calls and if you hear any screaming or loud noises coming from my office, ignore them."

Jackie smiled, "Yes, ma'am!"

Katie said, "What's up?"

"We are here on official business," Sydney said.

"You have been weighed in the balance and found wanting," Mackenzie said. "It's been noted that you have been working way too many hours and we are here to do something about it."

"Really? And just what do you propose we do?"

Mackenzie smiled. "We intend to kidnap you and take you clubbing tonight."

"Oh, I wish," Katie said. "But there's no way I can do it tonight. I've got an important meeting in three hours with Keith Mitchell, the president of Thackery Chemicals, and then an important staff meeting at three."

"That's terrible," Sydney said, smiling at Mackenzie.

"It sure is," Mackenzie said as she walked over to Katie's desk and hit the intercom. "Jackie, this is Mackenzie. Would you please call Keith Mitchell and let him know that Ms. Hamilton has taken ill and reschedule their meeting?"

Katie shot up out of her chair to object as Sydney slapped handcuffs on Katie's right wrist. "We can do this the hard way or you can make this a lot easier on yourself and cooperate. What's it going to be?"

Katie looked at her in shock and then at Mackenzie. They all stood in silence for a second and then Katie burst into laughter. "Okay, okay, I surrender." With the intercom still on Katie said, "Better do as you're told, Jackie. They have a gun and they're not afraid to use it. Clear my schedule for the rest of the day and until noon tomorrow."

Jackie was trying to contain her delight, "Okay, Katie. I certainly hope you're feeling better by tomorrow."

"Oh, I'm sure I'll be feeling terrific. Maybe a slight headache, but I'm positive it will be well worth it. Would you find Neal and ask him to come in here for a minute?"

Mackenzie said, "Now don't you feel better already? Your brother has taught me that it's okay to stop and smell the roses occasionally. The work will still be here when I get back and no one cares except yours truly that it didn't get done on time."

Katie was still giggling as Sydney unlocked the handcuffs from her wrist. "You're right, Mackenzie. Chad would be the first one to send me on my way. But I'll bet Keith Mitchell is going to be less than thrilled about this late cancellation." But then she said with a twinkle in her eye, "Maybe we could invite him along. He might enjoy the company of three lovely ladies." The girls did make a striking trio.

"I know I would!" Neal said as he walked into Katie's office.

"Neal!" Sydney and Mackenzie shouted in unison, each giving him a big hug.

Katie beamed as the girls kept doting over Neal. "I thought you might like to say hi to these girls, Neal. It's been a long time."

"It's been way too long," Sydney said.

"So what brings you lovely ladies to Hamilton Industries?"

"We came to kidnap Katie and go have some fun. Care to join us?" Mackenzie asked.

"That's a tempting offer, but no. Although I would like to be a fly on the wall and watch you girls. You're not going to do anything shameful are you?"

"Oh, I hope so," Sydney said as the other two giggled.

Katie said, "When's the last time you went clubbing, Neal?"

"Clubbing, what's clubbing?"

"Oh, Neal," Mackenzie replied. "You're hopeless. There are at least a dozen nightclubs in Cambridge alone." She looked at Katie and Sydney. "I'm thinking maybe we visit Toad. Whaddya think girls?"

Neal said. "What's a toad? I thought you were going out to a nightclub?"

Sydney stifled a laugh. "Toad is a nightclub. Dancing to a great DJ or live band is just what the doctor ordered."

"That settles it, Neal," Katie said. "You're coming with us. That's an order!"

"Whoa," Neal said. "I don't, or should I say, *can't* dance!"

"Well," Mackenzie said. "This is your lucky day."

Neal looked like he wanted to crawl into a hole and disappear.

Katie said, "Don't worry, Neal; we're going to have a great time."

"All right," Neal said. "But these are the only clothes I have." Neal was wearing a faded pair of jeans, a plaid long sleeved shirt with the sleeves rolled up to his elbows, and a pair of casual brown scuffed shoes with no socks. His hair was as it always looked, shaggy and at least two weeks overdue for a haircut.

"You have no other clothes?" Sydney asked incredulously.

"No, I have other clothes, but they all look like this." Neal looked a little sheepish and embarrassed.

"Okay," Katie said. "We are going to go home and get all dolled up. Then we'll come back here and pick you up. Hamilton Industries is going to buy you a new set of threads for tonight. While we're gone I want you to go to Chad's barber." She handed him a card. "I'll call him and tell him to give you the works. Then we are going to go shopping. You're going to look so amazing that all the women at Toad will be jealous that we are with such a handsome and available guy."

Neal just stood there shaking his head.

"You're just going to have to trust us, Neal," Mackenzie said. "Do you?"

"I do trust you ladies, but do I really have a choice?"

"There's always a choice, Neal," Katie said. "You can go with us or you're fired!"

Neal eyed all three of them, saying nothing. Then he finally shrugged his shoulders, smiled and said, "I'm yours."

———

WHILE MACKENZIE WAS at her condo getting ready for the evening out, her phone rang. She looked at the display and smiled. "Hello there, sailor. This is a pleasant surprise."

"Hi, Mac," Chad said. "I know its 2:00 in the afternoon there in Cambridge, but it's 5:00 a.m. here in Seoul."

"Why up so early?"

"You know me, Mac. I woke up about an hour ago and my brain immediately started working overtime. I was going to get up early anyway as I needed to talk to Neal. I'm going to bring him over tomorrow. I need him here. Whatever is going on at this juncture needs his brain and attention to detail. I was going to have him flown over here immediately until he told me of his plans for the evening. You girls really going to try and make a man out of him?"

"Neal is a man and don't you forget it, Mr. Hamilton. He just needs a little encouragement and some TLC with it. It's going to be fun."

Chad said, "You ladies don't plan on ditching your bodyguards, do you?"

"Not as long as they don't get in the way and spoil our fun."

"How can you have fun with me not there?"

"Hey, girls have got to have fun now and then. And since their boyfriends are ten thousand miles away, well, you know."

"Alright, you have fun and make sure I get poor Neal here all in one piece."

"Wouldn't have it any other way. Love you."

"Love you, too."

———

A SHORT TIME later the girls were back at Hamilton headquarters looking great and ready to party.

"Wow, look at you ladies. Are you sure you want to be seen with a skinny little computer geek like me?"

All three ladies looked in Neal's direction. Katie was the first to respond. "Well, well, mister. There's actually a handsome face under that mop of hair. Derek did a great job on you."

"I'll say," Sydney said.

Neal's hair was cleaned up and trimmed to a moderate length. It really did look good.

Mackenzie said, "Let's hurry over to Donato's and get you some threads. I think the world is ready to see the new Neal Sweeney, don't you?"

"Yes," Katie and Sydney replied in unison.

A submissive Neal said, "All right. Let's get this over with!"

———

DONATO'S WAS a respected men's clothier in Cambridge. The girls walked through the front doors, followed by a reconciled Neil who looked like he was being escorted to the principal's office. The sales clerk approached the girls with a big smile. "My name is Jon. Can I help you, ladies?"

"No," Mackenzie said as she grabbed Neal, proceeding to push him in front. "This is the young man we'd like you to assist. We are on our way to Toad. This is Neal and he would appreciate your expertise. I know that the attire for that establishment is casual but we'd like all eyes to be on Neal. Can you help him?"

Jon looked Neal over, "It would be my pleasure. I think what you need Neal is something in the casual nice category."

"Whatever," Neal stammered.

Jon and the girls were enjoying Neal's discomfort. "So, Neal," Jon said, "I'm sensing that you'd like to get this over ASAP, is that right?"

"Exactly."

Jon worked quickly and, with the help of three giddy ladies, Neal was looking good in no time at all. A half hour later Neal looked, as the girls put it, hot! He had on a brown, long-sleeved shirt under a light beige vest, skinny jeans and Kenneth Cole square-toed loafers, Neal was as ready as he was ever going to be.

"Jon, you did great," Katie said, as she handed him her American Express Gold Card.

The clerk beamed.

———

TOAD WAS A HAPPENING PLACE. Although not very large, it was arranged to take advantage of every inch. The tables were set in such a way that all could see the stage where a live band played every night. In order to get a seat you needed to arrive before 6:00 p.m. As Neal and the girls were being escorted to their table, three men at an adjacent table noticed them as they passed by.

"Hello, ladies!" one of them said. "You three look absolutely stunning." And they did. Although casually dressed, they nevertheless caught the eye of every gentleman nearby. But the man who spoke to them, and his two buddies, were by no means gentlemen. Noticing that Neal was with them he quipped, "Couldn't find a babysitter for little brother, huh?" He looked at his buddies who snickered.

Bending over the table, Sydney smiled. "You boys here for a good time?"

The apparent leader of the pack could hardly contain himself. "Yeah, baby!"

Sydney leaned closer and whispered in his ear. "Go home and take a shower then come back, you really stink. Maybe a change of diapers would also help."

The smile on his face slowly disappeared. Before he could say a word the women headed for their table, arm in arm with Neal.

"Forget what that idiot said about you. He's a complete jerk."

"It's okay, ladies. I'm sort of used to those kinds of comments."

"Not tonight, mister," Katie said. "You look like a million bucks. You're the man."

"Here, here," the girls said.

Neal's face turned a few shades of red.

———

A SHORT TIME LATER, Mackenzie said, "All right, Neal. The hour has arrived." She stood up and extended her hand. "Let's dance."

"Oh please, I can't."

"Sure you can, Neal," Katie said. "Look out there. Most people don't know what they're doing. They're just having fun." She pointed towards the stage. "Go!"

"All right, all right. I surrender." Neal got up and walked with Mackenzie towards the band. When they got there, Neal turned toward her and started rocking out. And he looked good.

"Look at that little beast. Can't dance?! He's been holding out on us."

Almost as if he could hear them Neal glanced over to the table with a smirk. When the song ended, Neal and Mackenzie came back to the table.

"You little devil," Sydney said. "You knew how to dance all along."

"Things are not always as they seem," Neal teased.

"What else don't we know about you?" Katie asked.

"Oh, no," Mackenzie groaned. "Here come those morons we encountered earlier. Probably full of liquor."

"Hello, ladies. Can we buy you a drink?"

Sydney said, "Did you go home and shower like I suggested?"

The leader said. "I'll forgive you for that if you'll dance with me. My name is Bill. What's yours?"

Neal said, "Why don't you boys go back to your table and order some coffee. You'll feel better."

"Well, well. Little brother has a voice. Bug off, little man."

Neal stood up and faced Bill. Even though he was five feet, eleven inches tall, and Bill was only an inch taller at six feet, Bill out weighed him by at least 100 pounds. Bill smiled and started to say something as he tapped Neal on the chest with his finger. In a flash, his hand had a handcuff on it. He was quickly whipped around and slammed face down on the table. As his arms were jerked behind him and the other cuff put on, Sydney said, "My name is Detective Nichols. You have two choices. Number one, you can apologize to Neal, or, number two, you can go to jail for disturbing a public event." She paused for a second. "What's it going to be?"

After what seemed to be an extremely long time, Bill came up and, turning towards Neal apologized.

"Good choice." She took off the cuffs. "Now you boys go back to your table and behave yourselves."

They turned to walk back as Bill looked at Neal. "You're lucky big sister was here to protect you." Sydney pushed him on his way.

"Don't let guys like that bother you, Neal. They're not worth it. Bullies are a dime a dozen."

Neal was dejected but smiled. "I'm okay, but I do have to go to the bathroom. Would you ladies excuse me?"

"Of course, Neal."

As Neal walked away the girls were frowning and feeling sorry for him. Because their heads were down a bit, they didn't notice Neal stop at the troublemakers' table. Neal leaned over and said something to Bill, then proceeded to the bathroom, but not before turning and saying one more thing to them. The three guys momentarily stared at each other in disbelief and then got up and headed for the bathroom, all without the girls noticing.

"I feel so bad for Neal," Mackenzie said. "It sounds like he's had his share of teasing in his life."

Katie was frowning. "Why do guys like that get their kicks from bullying someone who they feel is inferior to them?"

"Don't worry," Sydney said. "It's been my experience that sooner or later they'll get theirs." She glanced over at their table. "Well at least it looks like they left anyway."

Mackenzie said, "Good riddance." She looked towards the restroom area. "I hope Neal's okay." As she finished her sentence, a cold lump formed immediately in her stomach. "You don't think those thugs followed Neal into the bathroom?" All three stared at each other for a split second, and then snapped into action. But as they jumped up out of their chairs, they discovered it was too late.

Coming out of the bathroom with blood all over his vest, was Neal.

CHAPTER TWENTY

As THE GIRLS rushed to Neal, he held both arms up and hands open. "I'm okay. Let's get back to the table."

They quickly got hold of Neal and escorted him back to the table, then started peppering him with questions.

"Oh, Neal, what happened?"

"Are you all right?

"Who did this? Was it those three losers? We thought they'd left," Sydney said. "If we had known, we could've prevented it."

Neal calmly raised his hand to silence them. "I'm fine. I'm so sorry about the vest. When I invited Bill and his friends to join me in the bathroom, I didn't realize he was such a bleeder."

"You did what!?" Mackenzie nearly screamed.

Neal nodded.

All three ladies stared dumbfounded at Neal and said nothing.

So Neal elaborated. "When I walked by their table on the way to the bathroom, I leaned over and told Bill if he'd like to dance, I'd be in the bathroom."

The girls still said nothing as their mouths dropped open.

"Then as I left the table I turned and said to Bill, 'And why don't you bring your girlfriends with you?' "

That did it. Sydney said, "Do you have some kind of death wish, Neal?!"

As she finished her question, all three looked over to the bathroom door watching in disbelief as Bill and his buddies exited. Bill had a bunch of paper towels pressed against his nose with the front of his shirt covered in blood. Beside him was one of his associates holding up the third guy who had his arm around him and was limping badly. They were barely working their way towards Neal and the ladies.

"Oh, dear," Katie said.

Bill removed the paper towel from his broken nose. "Me and my friends would like to apologize for our rude behavior."

There were a few moments of excruciating silence as the girls were still in shock and were not processing the whole event.

Finally Neal broke the silence. "Why thank you, Bill. Your apology is appreciated. We accept." He let another couple of seconds go and then said, "You boys may go now."

Bill mumbled a *thank you* and they turned and walked away past their table and out the door.

As the ladies watched them leave they slowly turned, looking at each other and finally all eyes went to Neal.

Neal sat quietly enjoying the silence. Finally he said, "When I was 15 years old, I had already had my share of moments being bullied by bigger guys. I pretty much would go to my room and isolate myself. My computer and I became best friends. But my mother was concerned about my being alone all the time. Did I say concerned? She was beside herself. Even though my computer skills were better than anyone could imagine, my grades were in the toilet. I had no friends and I was becoming more and more secluded from everything and everyone. One day she expressed her concerns to our Pastor. He suggested that maybe what I needed was a little confidence. He referred her to one of his friends who happened to be an expert in martial arts. She talked to the friend and he invited her to bring me to his dojo."

Mackenzie said, "And the rest is history."

"Not by a long shot," Neal said. "I wasn't the least bit interested. I just wanted to be left alone and told her so. She respected my wishes and didn't bring it up again."

Katie said, "So what happened?"

"Brett Townsend."

"Who's Brett Townsend?"

"The last guy to ever beat me up. When I came home from school that day, my mom took one look at my swollen fat lip and my closed left eye and said, "That's it!" She dragged me down to the dojo and introduced me to Sato. At first I hated it and him. At age 15, I was five foot, one inch and weighed a whopping one hundred pounds. I resisted for a few weeks but gradually Sato won me over. I found that his form of karate, Shotokan, which originated in Okinawa in the eighteen hundreds, was more than just fighting. As I was learning skills in self-defense, I was also being taught the philosophy and principles of patience, humility, respect, compassion, and both an inward and outward calmness."

"How long did you do it?" Katie asked.

"I still am. It's been eleven years now. I'm actually a second degree black belt."

Mackenzie said, "Wow, I'm impressed." Mackenzie was somewhat of an expert in Taekwondo. "How often have you had to use it to defend yourself?"

"That was the first time," Neal said sheepishly.

"Why didn't you tell us before. We thought you were in serious trouble?"

Neal smiled. "I wanted to surprise you."

"Well you certainly did that," Sydney said. "What happened in the bathroom?"

"Bill walked in a little ahead of his boys and told me I had a lot of nerve putting myself in a position to get my butt kicked. I tried to reason with him but it was no use. He used a few expletives about my ancestry."

Katie interrupted. "You mischievous sprite! You knew that by getting them into the bathroom it had to end the way it did."

"You're right," Neal said. "It hurt to see the way you all felt so bad for me because of those guys. I decided it was time to teach them some manners and redeem myself with three lovely ladies."

"You certainly did that," Mackenzie said. She looked at Katie and Sydney. "Shall we go tell our bodyguards to take the night off? I suddenly feel very protected."

They laughed as Mackenzie looked at Neal. "So, we are dying to know, finish the bathroom account, please."

"Yes, please," said Katie and Sydney.

"Not much to tell. It really ended almost before it started. After Bill taught me a few new words that made my toes curl, he saw that I was smiling, which irritated him to no end. As he reached back to hit me, which was an easy read, I shoved the palm of my hand through his nose, and then quickly whirled around and drove my foot into the second guy's knee. As I turned to the other guy he immediately brought up his hands in a gesture of surrender, which I thought was nice. I told him to help his buddy who was writhing in pain on the ground while I got some wet paper towels to help Bill, who, by then, was bleeding profusely. I'm so sorry about the vest."

"Don't worry about it," Katie said. "It was well worth it."

"Anyway, I told Bill that I would appreciate it if he and his buddies would apologize to you and then leave. I also might have mentioned that if they didn't, I would be very disappointed."

Sydney grinned. "Can't dance or fight, huh, Neal? What else are we going to find out about you."

"Can I see your gun?" Neal asked.

For the second time that night Sydney's mouth fell open.

"Just kidding," Neal laughed. "I hate guns."

"Who needs them?" Katie remarked. "We've got Neal!"

134

CHAPTER TWENTY-ONE

Twenty-four hours later, the Hamilton jet landed at the Seoul airport. It was four in the morning and Neal was definitely feeling it. Chad smiled as Neal departed the jet. "Hey, champ, how's it going?"

Neal yawned. "Considering I've been on this flight for over sixteen hours, and that I lost almost thirty hours in the time zone changes, I'm doing okay. How long did it take you to get over the jet lag?"

"I'll let you know when it happens," Chad said smiling.

"Ugh! That bad?"

"Our hours haven't been normal since we arrived four days ago. And, we haven't made much progress either." Chad helped Neal load his one suitcase in the trunk of his Army issue car. "We're going to have a brainstorming session later this morning to bring you up to date. Hopefully the five of us can come up with some ideas that will get us closer to who's behind all of this."

"All of what?" Neal asked.

"We're not sure of that either. We know that part of it is drugs, but there may be more to it."

"You said the five of us?"

"That's right. You don't know about Bo Davies. The CIA has assigned him to us. Since Peter Strickland is a wanted man in the United States and abroad, the FBI and CIA are cooperating on this one."

"Are you still in charge?"

Chad smiled and grimaced at the same time. "That I am, if you could call it that. Right now we are a little frustrated. Hopefully you can help us tie everything together."

"Piece of cake," Neal said sarcastically.

———

"Welcome aboard, Killer," Kade said as he grabbed Neal's suitcase out of the car.

Neal gave Kade a half smile but said nothing.

Extending his hand Bo Davies introduced himself to Neal.

Neal said, "Chad told me about you on the way. Happy to meet you."

"Nice to have someone around whom I can have an intelligent conversation with," Chad said.

"Hey!" Kade protested.

"I hope that doesn't include me," Ender said as he approached Neal. "Glad to have you here, young man. Are you here to help us solve this mess or just protection?"

"I guess you all heard about my little encounter yesterday at the Toad."

"The Toad?" Kade asked. "I thought you were at a nightclub with the ladies?"

"The Toad is a nightclub, you big dummy," Chad teased. "You need to get out more."

"That would be a lot easier if I wasn't working for a slave driver like you," Kade countered.

"Anyway," Ender said, "It's good to have you with us. Why don't you get cleaned up and then we'll go over to the mess hall and grab some breakfast. The cuisine here is not too bad."

"Sounds good. I could use a shower and some food."

Chad said. "Good, and then we'll get started and fill you in on where we are."

"Or where we aren't," Kade groaned.

———

"So what do you have so far?" Neal asked, as he took a bite of his breakfast sausage.

"Only a lot of suspicion," Chad said. "We've done a pretty thorough search of the base. Everything seems to be in order. Somehow they're doing this operation right under our noses. While we continue our investigation I need you to work your computer skills on the four suspects that we've discussed. We don't have their passwords for their computers but…"

"That won't be necessary," Neal said.

"I didn't think so," Chad smiled.

Chad looked at the others. "Okay, boys, what are we missing? We know that drugs are originating from this base and ending up in Newfoundland."

Ender said, "We haven't found anything out of place or even remotely suspicious. No unusual containers, nothing hidden inside of containers, and nothing out of the ordinary."

"So, again I say, what are we missing?"

Kade said, "Hiding in plain sight."

They all stared at Kade and said nothing.

"Maybe we're looking too hard. Usually in scenarios like this, the truth ends up being right in front of our eyes." He looked at Chad. "In Africa, how many times were we looking for something that turned out to be right under our noses?"

Chad said, "More often than not." He paused. "Okay, let's think about this. What is the main commodity that moves out of this base to Newfoundland?"

"Troops." Ender said. "The men returning home from all of Asia come through this base."

Bo said, "Obviously all these thousands of men aren't involved. That would be impossible."

"Right you are, Bo," Chad said. "There's no way all those men would knowingly transport illegal drugs. So, where does that leave us? If they aren't involved, what else gets transported?"

Ender said, "Not much. Some food and a few supplies, but they all checked out. No impropriety there."

"Gotta be the troops' duffle bags."

All eyes turned to Kade. "It's the only logical answer. Let's say you're transporting a little over 200 soldiers per trip. What do they all carry with them? Their duffle bags."

"Your theory has merit, Kade," Chad said. "But how?"

"Maybe a false bottom," Ender said.

"Okay. But we know that when the troops arrive, their bags are legitimate. How would they make the switch without them knowing?" Chad asked.

Bo said, "And when? Aren't those bags with them most of the time or at least in or near their bunks; the logistics would be a nightmare. And the bags would be unguarded at different times. There's just no way."

"When are the bags all together?" Kade asked.

"In the baggage compartment when they're loaded onto the air transport. Not a lot of time," Chad said. "But possibly doable. They'd have to be extremely efficient, which drug operations usually are. So that gives us the possibility of the *when*, but we still don't have the *how*."

Bo said, "When is the next movement of troops to Newfoundland?"

"Day after tomorrow at 6:00 a.m." Chad said. "What do you think?"

Ender said, "I think it's weak, but I've seen a lot weaker in my years with the Bureau."

"All right," Chad said. "It is a little far-fetched. We'll keep looking and in the meantime, our suspicions stay here in this room, got it?"

All nodded.

CHAPTER TWENTY-TWO

THIRTY-SIX HOURS LATER...

"CHAD, YOU'RE A GENIUS," Kade said.

"*Au contraire,* my friend. You are the one who suggested that they might be operating in plain sight."

"That's true. Hard to be modest sometimes. Anyway, we got 'em. Let's go inform the General and wrap this thing up. Peter Strickland is waiting for us in Rio."

Chad said, "You're right."

Ender said. "I agree. Let's end this."

"Agreed," Bo said.

"GOOD MORNING, GENERAL," Chad said as Lieutenant Bowers escorted our four heroes into General Markum's office.

"I hear you have some good news for me, gentlemen." Markum said.

"That we do," Chad said.

"Please, sit down," Markum said as Lt. Bowers arranged some chairs around his desk.

"What have you got?"

Kade laid three photographs on General Markum's desk. They showed two men doing something to the duffle bags in the air transport's cargo hold.

Kade said, "These were taken this morning. As you will note, Sergeant Miller and Corporal Thompson with the help of two other Privates, are removing the straps on the duffel bags and replacing them with new ones. They were very efficient and did it within 30 minutes."

Chad removed a strap from a bag that he'd been carrying. You'll notice that this strap is fatter than your usual ones. Underneath is a special zipper that when opened reveals several bags of heroin. Multiply that by over two hundred and you have approximately a street value of over 800 thousand dollars. Multiply that by four times each month and you can see that you have a major operation going, worth millions of dollars."

Markum sat silently for a moment. "I can't believe that something as simple as a strap could bring in that kind of money." He paused again for a second and then said, "Do you know who the brains are behind this operation?"

Chad said, "First of all, let me introduce you to our very special computer expert, Neal Sweeney." Neal smiled sheepishly. "General, I'm sorry to say that your computer has been hacked to make it look like you are behind all of this."

"What! Who? The only person who has access to my computer is Lieutenant Bowers." He looked at Bowers. "Bobby, what do you have to say?"

Bowers said, "I have no idea what's going on. I swear I don't know anything about this!" He looked at Chad.

Ender said, "You're right, Lieutenant." He looked at the General. "Isn't he, General?"

"Are you suggesting that I know something about this? I'd tread lightly if I were you, mister."

Chad said, "Without Neal, you might've gotten away with this. You even had Lieutenant Bowers as your fall guy."

General Markum glanced at Neal and then at Bowers, who looked totally bewildered.

"You see, General Markum; I know you make a pretty good salary as a General. Your stateside account shows that. And your retirement is more than adequate, but that wasn't enough, was it?"

Markum said nothing.

"A little cross checking shows some interaction between that account and an account here at the Bank of Seoul under the name of Greg Benjamin. It's a pretty hefty amount and shows regular deposits to your account in the United States."

"I have no idea what you're talking about. Even if it were true, it's all circumstantial."

Kade said, "You're right about that, General. Here's another bit of circumstantial evidence. The Greg Benjamin account here in Seoul shows deposits of close to a million dollars over the past two years, which were immediately transferred to an account in the Cayman Islands."

"More circumstantial evidence," the General said.

"True," Chad said, "but more than enough to put you under a military court martial. We aren't here as a police force, just a fact finding mission. Your operation has been shut down. Whoever is in Newfoundland will be arrested in a couple of hours when they attempt to switch the straps back. The authorities have been contacted, including the CIA and Special Agent Brimhall's superior at the FBI. There are enough facts so far to satisfy your superiors to put you under arrest. There are two MP's outside your door to detain you until a full court martial can be set up." Chad nodded to Bo to send in the MP's.

General Markum said nothing. He sat quietly while the MP's were escorted into the General's office. Then a slight smile began to form. "Very good, Mr. Hamilton. You and your extremely capable team are to be commended for a job well done."

Chad felt his stomach turn. Something wasn't right.

Markum said, "Let me introduce you to part of my team that you haven't met yet." With that the two MP's took out their guns along with Lieutenant Bowers and pointed them at Chad and his team.

"Well, well, we didn't see that one coming," Kade said sarcastically.

"Always have a plan B and an escape set up," Markum said. "I have to hand it to you, Chad. Peter said you boys would get to the bottom of our little operation but I had no idea you'd be so successful this fast."

Chad said. "You do realize that we've already been in touch with our contacts at the FBI and CIA and, even though you were supposed to be arrested by your goons here, that it's only a matter of time before they realize something has gone wrong and will be here in full force?"

"Nice try, Hamilton. I know for a fact that you just discovered the drugs on the transport early this morning and that you boys came straight here to report your findings to me."

Kade said, "So now what, General? Do we face the proverbial firing squad?"

"Don't be so melodramatic, Kade. Peter would have my head if anything happened to you and Chad. His fun is just beginning. A few days in the stockade while we finish up here and join Peter in Rio will suffice. I'm sure you geniuses will figure a way to get out eventually. By then we will be long gone."

Ender said, "You're a disgrace to that uniform, General Markum, and everyone will know it soon."

Markum looked sternly at Ender, "Be very careful what you say to me, Agent Brimhall. Peter Strickland doesn't care what I do to you, Mr. Davies, and your very proficient computer expert. I haven't decided what to do with you three, but I assure you it won't be pleasant. In answer to your statement, you're right, I will go down as a disgrace as far as the Army is concerned, but seeing as I have no family back home and neither do any of my handpicked cohorts in crime, we decided long ago that living the rest of our lives in a remote location with all the money we need to live like kings would be sufficient."

The MP's and Lieutenant Bowers had already disarmed Chad and his team. "Before my men escort you gentlemen to your new quarters, I'll have all your cell phones." All five gave up their phones. "Frisk them for anything else that might be useful," General Markum said.

———

"This seems to happen every time we get a little cocky, doesn't it?" Kade said to Chad.

"Got that right."

Ender said, "Don't beat yourself up, Chad. None of us saw this coming. We all underestimated Markum's operation." He stood up from his bunk and looked around. "I don't see an easy way out of here."

Kade said, "Getting out of this match box isn't the problem. It's the guard outside the door. We need to come up with a plan to distract him."

All eyes moved to Chad.

"What!?"

"You're the brains behind this operation," Kade teased. "I thought by now you'd have several scenarios as to how to get out of here."

"I do, but they all go out the window with that guard outside the door. What we need is someone on the outside. Too bad that cute little detective of yours wasn't close by. We could sure use Sydney right about now."

They all nodded but said nothing.

A smile began to form on Neal's face. Chad finally noticed. "Something humorous about all of this, Mr. Sweeney?"

Neal said. "I just thought it was ironic that you should mention how Sydney could be a big help if she were here."

Kade said, "Neal, you're an amazing man, a genius as a matter of fact. But even you can't transport Sydney half way around the world in five minutes."

"Oh ye of little faith," Neal quipped. "I can do exactly that."

Nobody said anything. Chad finally said. "What's going on Neal?"

"Sydney is here."

––––––––

KADE SHOT up from his bunk. "What!? How?"

"She came with me two days ago."

Chad said, "Why?"

"She and Mackenzie said they..."

"Mackenzie, too!" Chad screamed. "Why didn't you tell us?"

"They wanted to surprise you."

"Well they certainly did that. Where are they?" Chad asked.

"They're staying at the Marriott in downtown Seoul."

Kade said, "This is all well and good but there's still one minor little challenge."

Chad said, "How do we contact them so they can get in touch with our assets."

"Right you are, buddy. So Neal, unless you got some little gadget that transfers our brain waves to theirs, we're screwed."

Neal smiled again. "How about a cell phone?"

They all said nothing.

Neal looked up at the surveillance camera. "They're watching us but I'm almost certain they have no sound. They're more concerned with what we're doing rather than what we are saying. I have a cell phone in a little pocket in the crotch of my pants."

Kade said, "Why, Neal, you little devil."

"If I reach in and get it, we'll be found out. What we need is a distraction while I go directly under the camera, get it out and make the call or text them."

Chad said, "Great job, Neal. Okay, here's what we're going to do. Ender, you and Bo get into an animated discussion that will eventually escalate into an actual fight. Then the rest of us will jump up and try to break it up. Neal, you'll sneak over and text the girls. I'm not totally convinced that we're not bugged so texting will be better. Tell them to get in touch with the FBI at the Boston Regional Center. They know the Director there and he'll know what to do. Tell them that under no circumstances are they to get involved any further; that it's too dangerous and that we are being detained but not in any immediate danger. Got it?"

"Got it," Neal said.

On Chad's signal Ender and Bo went into action. Once they came at each other in an apparent fight, Chad and Kade jumped in to try and stop them while Neal inched his way under the camera, pulled out the phone, and began texting. He did it quickly and hit send. Within a minute he got an answer. "Okay, he shouted. It's done."

Once Chad and Kade had broken up the staged fight, they all returned to their respective bunks and lay still for a few minutes pretending to cool off.

"Do you think we pulled it off?" asked Ender.

Bo was rubbing his jaw. "As far as I'm concerned you did."

"Sorry about that, Bo. I thought you were going to back up, not lean in."

Kade said, "I think you guys did great. I'm sure they'd be in here by now if they thought we were up to something."

"I agree," Chad said. "I wonder what the FBI will be able to do. There's a lot of politics involved here. Even though South Korea is one of our allies, I don't know how excited they'd be about storming a US Army base."

Kade said, "We still need to come up with some kind of a plan soon. Don't forget, Bo, Ender and Neal are not out of the woods.

They could still bring a world of hurt on them. How about when they bring us dinner?"

Chad said, "I was thinking the same thing, Kade. And we do have an ace up our sleeve."

"What's that?" Bo asked.

Chad smiled, "Neal!"

CHAPTER TWENTY-THREE

"You mean *Killer*," Kade teased.

Neal's face turned a fine shade of red.

"How do we use Neal to our advantage?" Ender questioned.

"We all have to admit, including you, Neal, that you aren't the most imposing looking person in the world."

Chad said, "You're right about that, Kade. When they bring the food through the door, he could timidly walk up to grab the tray. As soon as he takes it, Neal disables the soldier before he knows what hit him. Then we rush the other guy as he is momentarily surprised by Neal's expertise."

"I like it," Bo said. "When do you think they'll bring dinner?"

"I'd say most likely two or three hours from now."

"Okay," Chad said. "Since we've got the time let's see if we can refine this and eliminate all scenarios as best we can."

———

About two and a half hours later, they heard footsteps outside coming towards their building.

Chad said, "This is it, boys. We only get one shot at this so don't mess up."

"Speak for yourself, Cupcake," Kade said as he positioned himself at the edge of his bunk, closest to the door."

Neal got up and casually stood about six feet from the door.

A key entered the lock and a metal bar was removed from two reinforced brackets and the door opened.

Neal casually took a leisurely step towards the door, which was now slowly opening. Chad, Bo, Kade, and Ender leaned forward ready to pounce.

But the MP wasn't holding a tray of food. He had a strange look on his face as he was shoved into the room. Behind him stood the other MP with his hands up and behind him with a rifle in her hands was a smiling Sydney. Next to her as they entered through the door, also with a rifle in hand, was Mackenzie, also with a jovial look on her face.

"What the...?" Chad mumbled as Mackenzie interrupted.

"Well hello, sailor; fancy running into you boys all the way here in Seoul, Korea."

Chad's puzzled look quickly turned to irritation as he looked to Neal, who shrugged his shoulders as if to say, *I delivered your message.*

Kade was the first to recover. He took the rifle from Sydney, ordered the two soldiers face down on the floor and hugged Sydney with his free arm, then said, "Nice to see you, Syd. What took you so long?"

Chad was trying to maintain his angry look but couldn't help himself and broke into a big grin. "My hero," he said as he threw his arms around Mackenzie. "We'll discuss your actions later but right now we need to get out of here pronto. I assume these gentlemen were the guards at the front gate."

The women nodded. "We have their jeep about 50 feet from here."

"Okay, let's get off this base as fast as we can. We'll deal with the

General later. If we can get to the gate and onto the road outside of the base we'll be home free. As soon as we are in the jeep, Ender you call the Director. He should be able to get some action and with the cooperation of Bo's friends at the CIA, we ought to be in a safe house soon. Any questions?"

No one spoke.

"Alrighty then, let's vacate this place!"

———

Hey Doug,

Oh man, the things that have happened since we last talked. Right now I'm at the Marriott in Seoul, South Korea, relaxing with Kade, Ender, Bo, Neal, and, oh yes, Mackenzie and Sydney. I'm afraid I have to admit it, the girls saved our butts on this one. I got a little over confident and we ended up in the brig. I'm still a little peeved that they showed up unannounced; at least I'm pretending to be, but now that this part of our mission is over we are enjoying one whole day of R & R. Then it's back to work and off to Rio, where I'm almost certain we'll find Peter Strickland. Right now I'm assuming that General Markum and his band of merry men are being taken care of. Even if they get away, the operation is shut down and the Army has all the info they need on him and most of those that are involved. That ought to make Peter take notice that I'm on to him and closing in. But then again, I'm pretty sure he knows that already. I think he wants to gradually reel me in, do as much damage to my friends and family as he can, and then have the final confrontation; him or me. I plan on it being him!

———

CHAD SAID, "Here's what I'm proposing; an early dinner at one of Seoul's finest, a show on Seoul's version of Broadway, back here for a great night's sleep, and then tomorrow off to Rio."

"Sounds like a plan to me," Kade said. "But instead of a show maybe we take in a fight."

Sydney said, "Oh, Michael, you are hopeless. A little culture won't hurt you."

"What's with the 'Michael'?" Neal asked.

"Kade's full name is Jacob Michael Kincaid," Chad said. "So Sydney calls him Michael; isn't that cute?"

Mackenzie playfully shoved Chad. "Watch it, Hamilton, or I'll tell everyone what my nickname is for you."

There were a few giggles as Kade said, "Yeah, Cupcake. Watch your mouth."

———

THE GANG of seven were seated at one of the best French Restaurants in Seoul: A Table.

Bo said, "Wow this is nice, Chad. How did you know about this place?"

"I did what any red blooded American would do."

"What he's trying to say," Mackenzie said, "is he Googled it."

Kade said, "Whatever, I'm impressed and I'm starving. How do you say bear in French or Korean? We could use Lieutenant Bowers right now. I was sorry that boy was a part of that operation."

"Me too," Chad said. "You just never know. He certainly had us all fooled."

Kade said, "It just goes to show you, you can't judge a leopard by his stripes."

Ender laughed. "I think you mean by his spots, don't you, Kade?"

Kade countered, "In Bower's case it *was* stripes!

———

AFTER A GREAT DINNER, they were enjoying a crêpe dessert with coffee.

Mackenzie said, "So tomorrow we're off to Rio. I wish it were under better circumstances."

"I shouldn't even let you two go," Chad lamented, "after what you pulled here."

Sydney smiled. "Be careful, mister. As cute as they are, someone had to save your sorry derrières."

"Admit it, Chad, we needed saving. I for one am extremely happy they did."

"Amen," Ender said. "Don't forget the General was going to let you and Kade go, but he hadn't decided what to do with Bo, Neal, and me."

"Here, here," Neal said.

"I know, I know" Chad said, "It's just that if anything happened to you two," he paused, "Kade would be terribly upset."

They all burst out laughing as Mackenzie nearly shoved Chad off of his chair.

Bo asked, "Chad, how do you know that Peter Strickland is in Rio de Janeiro?"

"I don't know for absolute certainty, but when I talked to him on the phone two weeks ago..."

Mackenzie gasped. "You what!?"

Chad smiled sheepishly. "I thought I told you about that, Mac."

Mackenzie shook her head.

"Well I meant to."

Mackenzie tilted her head down, her eyes still looking straight at Chad.

"Sorry. As I was saying, Bo," Chad tried to ignore Mackenzie's steely-eyed stare. "When Kade and I went to confront Arthur Wainwright we found him to be quite dead, so before the police arrived we took his cell phone. There was a certain number that was used quite often. We later found it to be a Rio number. Then when we apprehended the jerk that tried to kill my grandparents at the airport, lo and behold, guess who called his phone a minute later?"

Bo said, "Strickland."

"Bingo. We exchanged niceties; he saying he was going to destroy me and my family and, of course, I reciprocated and told him I was going to kill him." Chad sat in contemplation. "He's there all right. I know it, and when I find him we'll either get him extradited back to the United States or..."

"We end it right there," Kade said.

BOOK THREE

THE FIND

CHAPTER TWENTY-FOUR

CHAD's little posse of seven took a commercial flight to Galeão International Airport in the city of Rio de Janeiro. There was no need to have the Hamilton corporate jet come to Seoul to pick them up. Since his drug operation in Seoul had been shut down, Peter knew they were coming, which was fine with him. *A little game of cat and mouse until we meet face to face and we end it.* Or, as he was really thinking, *until I end it!*

After a long tedious thirteen-hour trip, they landed at the Galeão Airport. Chad had booked them rooms at the Caracas Rio Hotel. After a few hours of rest they came together in the hotel restaurant for a light brunch. After some pleasantries Chad said, "Okay, let's get started. Neal, what have you got?" Chad had assigned Neal to start the search for Strickland when they were on the flight to Rio.

"Actually, quite a bit."

Kade said, "Why am I not surprised? What did he have for breakfast, Neal?"

"Funny, Mr. Kincaid. Chad suggested that I look into the casinos and resorts."

Chad said, "Peter liked the good guy image. He worked hard for it all those years in Boston. I'm assuming he'll try and do the same here. I imagine he'll first work on his appearance. Unlike the movies where plastic surgeons can make you look like someone else, in reality they can only do so much. Maybe change the nose, raise the eyebrows, smooth some wrinkles, things like that. Since he had a nice head of hair I would think he probably shaves his head too."

"Even though we took some of his money he still has lots. A casino would be the way to go. There are so many ways to make money in gambling, legal and not so legal. So what have you got, Neal?"

"Three possibilities. Most casinos have been owned and operated by the same individuals or corporations for years. They don't change hands very often; too lucrative. There are two that have changed ownership in the last two or three years. If Peter were trying to expand his sphere of influence and empire, this would be a good way to go."

Ender said, "What about the third casino?"

"That would be the one I would choose to investigate first. A new casino and resort that began operations about three-and-a-half months ago," Neal said.

Chad said, "The timeline certainly fits. Who owns it?"

"A corporation of course."

Kade said, "What's the name?"

"Golden Resorts. They're out of Miami."

Kade said, "That sure sends up bells. Miami is Paul Stevens aka Peter Strickland's stomping grounds. Good work young man. What's the name of the resort?"

"Rio Cabuçu Casino and Resort."

"What's a kabookoo?" Mackenzie asked.

Neal said, "It's the main river that runs through Rio de Janeiro."

Chad said, "Okay, so we have a place to start. Ender, why don't you and Bo pick one of the other two casinos and start there tonight? Kade, the girls, and I will start with the Rio Cabuçu. We'll meet back at my room at about midnight. Keep your eyes and ears open and have some fun. Your losses are on me, up to a point. Fortunately I'll have Kade with me so I can keep an eye on him."

Kade said, "How much can I lose?"

"A buck fifty," Chad teased.

———

"Wow. Vegas has nothing on this casino," Sydney whispered.

Kade said, "This is going to be fun!"

"Down boy! Remember why we're here. Stay on your toes and keep alert."

"Maybe you haven't noticed, but I can do that and have fun, which is exactly what I intend to do. So, Syd, care to join me at the craps table? Let's see if I can lose that buck fifty."

Mackenzie said, "Chad, why don't you and I go see if the gentleman dealer at the blackjack table is talkative?"

"Are you ready for this?"

"Ready as I'll ever be. Let's do it."

———

"CAN YOU SMELL IT?" Bo said.

"Smell what?" asked Ender.

"Money! This is where I live. I love casinos."

"Hold on there, partner. We've got a job to do. Keep your eyes and ears open, remember. Let's see what we can find out about the ownership at this joint."

"Okay, but there's no reason I can't relieve them of some of their cash at the same time. You go ahead and move around. I'm going to find the room where the real high rollers are and play some poker."

Ender said, "Are you any good at it?"

"Some of my buddies at the company have nicknamed me *Cool Hand Luke* after I cleaned their clock."

"Just be careful."

Bo said, "Don't worry about me, Junior, you just take care of yourself and don't let the big boys hurt you."

Ender was irritated by Bo's comment but let it ride. He turned and headed for the roulette wheel.

Bo moved toward an employee who was standing with his arms folded, looking menacing, which was a big part of his job. "Excuse me, my good man. I'm looking to play a little poker."

The big guy pointed to a table about thirty feet away.

Bo said, "I'm sorry, I guess I wasn't clear enough." He pulled out a big wad of cash. "I'm looking for the real game."

The employee smiled. "Let me check and see if there might be a spot for you at the table. I'll be right back." He strolled over to another big guy who turned and walked through a door that was closed to the public. About a minute later he returned, said something to the first guy, who turned and walked back to Bo.

"If you'll follow me, sir, I think we can accommodate you."

Bo smiled and followed him into the room.

———

CHAD SAT at the blackjack table. Mackenzie stood behind his right shoulder to observe. The dealer noticed her and smiled. "Would you like to play?" he asked her.

"No thanks, I'm just going to make sure he doesn't lose all our money."

Chad said, "Wait a minute, little missy. I'm feeling lucky tonight. How about some chips. He handed the dealer $500 dollars and received his chips. He started out slow and bet fifty dollars. His first two cards were a five of clubs and a seven of diamonds, totaling twelve. The dealer's two cards totaled fourteen so Chad had to play. He drew an eight of clubs, totaling twenty. The dealer drew a queen of spades.

"Winner to the gentleman with the pretty lady."

Chad said, "All right, I told you this was going to be my night."
He bet one hundred dollars and won again.

"Wow, Mr. Hamilton. You certainly are lucky. Maybe I'll keep
you."

Chad continued his winning ways for the next hour and was up
over twenty-five thousand.

By now the dealer was calling Chad by his first name. "Wow,
Chad. Don't you think maybe you should quit and enjoy your
winnings?"

"Nice try, Bob. I'm just getting started. Deal 'em!"

"As he gave Chad his first card he said, "What's your secret,
Chad?"

"It's easy; I cheat."

CHAPTER TWENTY-FIVE

WHILE BO WAS in the back room playing in his high stakes poker game, Ender was enjoying himself at the craps table. He started a conversation with the man playing next to him. He said, "Nice establishment. Do you come here often?"

He was an older gentleman, approximately in his sixties, wearing some beige chinos and a blue polo. "Whenever I'm here in Rio, which is quite often, this is one of my favorite spots. They run a nice operation here, honest and clean. I usually do fairly well here. I actually like almost all the casinos in Rio."

"Almost all?" Ender asked.

"Yeah, there's a pretty new casino down the road called Rio Cabuçu that I don't frequent anymore."

"Oh, why is that?"

"I can't really say for sure. It just doesn't feel right somehow. For one thing I never seem to have any luck there. And for another thing, their managers all look like thugs from a mafia movie. You know, big, imposing, almost daring you to win. It just made me feel uneasy. I come to these places to relax and have fun you know. If you're going to take my money, at least let me enjoy it."

Ender said, "Thanks for the heads-up. I'll avoid that one."

"Maybe it's just me," the gentleman said. "You should at least give them a try. I'll tell you something; Rio Cabuçu is one of the most impressive casinos I've ever seen. Las Vegas pales in comparison!"

In the adjoining room, Bo was caught up in his fourth game of poker. So far he was a little behind but holding his own. He was an excellent poker player. His years with the CIA had enhanced his ability to read people's faces under stressful circumstances, and poker was no exception. While the dealer was shuffling the cards for their next game, the owner of the casino actually entered the room and looked around. Noticing Bo he strolled over to the table, extending his hand. "I'm Jud Peralta, owner of this recreational haven; welcome!"

"Thanks, I'm Bo Davies, here getting some R & R. I have interest in several companies in Rio. I have a soft spot for poker and am enjoying your establishment. But I have to warn you, I'm very good at this little game and my intentions are not honorable."

Peralta gave a hearty laugh. "Well you enjoy yourself, Mr. Davies. It's a pleasure taking your money, er, I mean, having your business."

Davies also laughed. "I like your attitude, Jud. Maybe we can have a drink later."

"Sounds good. It's on me, unless you do so well I can't afford it."

———

CHAD WAS NOW UP over $30,000 dollars. A crowd was starting to gather behind him. Even the dealer was smiling and getting into it. That is until he noticed Bret Sonjen standing off to the side. Bret was the so-called floor manager. Like most of the employees dressed in tuxedos, he was very imposing at 6'6", weighing in at approximately 260 and not an ounce of fat on him. He didn't look happy.

Chad won the next two hands. Sonjen had seen enough. He calmly walked over to Chad, leaned over close to his ear. "Our manager, Mr. Jaxocs would like a word with you in his office. Would you please come with me?"

Chad said, "As you can see I'm a little busy and having a wonderful time. Tell your Mr. Jaypoop or whatever his name is I'll see him a little later."

By now the crowd had noticed the commotion between the two men. "Leave him alone," shouted one of them.

"Yeah," shouted another. "Don't like it when someone is beating the house?!"

Others joined in. The big guy stepped back and said nothing.

Chad continued to play and was up $50,000 when the dealer got a nod from the imposing floor manager. He said, "I need to close down for fifteen minutes. Got a terrific headache. I'll be right back." The crowd again balked but Chad held up his hand to silence them.

"I need a short break myself." He turned to the big guy. "You got a name?"

"Bret."

"Well, Bret, if your manager would still like to meet me, I'd be tickled pink."

He looked at Chad a little amazed and with a tiny bit of admiration, but only a little. "If you'll follow me, sir."

"I'd be delighted." He smiled at Mackenzie as she took his arm. She looked a little concerned as Bret spoke.

"The nice lady can wait out here."

Mackenzie squeezed Chad's arm tight. Chad patted her hand and said. "It's okay, Mac. I won't be long. I'm just going to be a few minutes, isn't that right, Bret?"

Bret nodded. "Absolutely."

Mackenzie let go of Chad's arm reluctantly. Chad and his escort, who looked like a poster child for steroids, walked towards a closed door at the side of the main lounge. As he entered he couldn't help but notice all the monitors on the wall directly behind a large black desk. The man sitting at the desk didn't get up and showed a somber expression on his face. Like Bret, you could tell he was oversized and looked like he spent a lot of time in the weight room. He pointed to a chair across from his desk. "Sit down please."

He looked at Chad for a few seconds without changing his expression. Then a smile developed. "You're having a nice little run at the blackjack table, aren't you? I've been watching you on this monitor. You are very good. I mean, I'm very good at ferreting out cheaters, and, I have to admit, I can't see how you are doing it. I know you're counting cards but I don't see any devices and you don't look like a brainiac. So, tell me, Mr...."

"Hamilton, Chad Hamilton."

"Tell me, Mr. Hamilton, how do you do it?"

Chad said, "Superior technology." Chad reached into his ear and delicately pulled out a tiny device. "Bet you haven't seen one of these before." He handed it to Jaxocs.

Jaxocs smiled as he shook his head. "Amazing."

"Also, the second button here on my shirt is a microphone."

"I am impressed. Where's the camera?"

"My lady friend's pendant."

"So, Chad, is it okay if I call you Chad?"

"Absolutely, if I can call you..."

"Ted. Please do."

"So, Chad, are you completely nuts or just suicidal? You come in here bragging about how well you cheat. You have to know that you're not leaving with that fifty grand and that we could easily break every bone in your body. Then there's no telling what we could do to your lady friend out there."

"The fifty grand is a present. That was my way of getting in here to see you." Jaxocs looked slightly bewildered. "As far as breaking every bone in my body, take a look at the monitor that shows the area just outside your door. See that gentleman standing there, in the Hawaiian shirt? That's my partner. His name is Kade and if I don't let him know I'm okay, within ten minutes of my entering here, which by the way, is in three more minutes, he's going to come in and create all kinds of havoc. He's ex-CIA and is an expert in hand-to-hand combat, can shoot a fly off a glass 30 yards away, can make short work of you two, and is almost as good as I am. Lastly, you make any more threats regarding my lady and Kade and I will take turns on you two."

Chad let what he said sink in while Jaxocs said nothing.

"Now here's what you are going to do, Ted. Deliver a message from me to your boss, Peter Strickland."

You could have knocked Jaxocs over with a feather. After he regained his composure, the smile he had at the beginning returned. "I have to hand it to you, Hamilton. You are everything that Peter said you were. How did you know this was his operation?"

Chad said, "Tell your boss that Neal found him. He'll know who I'm talking about. He's already cost Strickland two hundred seventy-five million dollars!"

"Well, Chad, I didn't think that you could do this so quick, but Peter did."

"What do you mean?" Chad asked.

Jaxocs reached into the top drawer of his desk and pulled out an envelope. "This is for you."

The envelope was sealed but on the outside was written *To My Friend Chad Hamilton.*

With that, Ted Jaxocs stood up. "You're free to go, Mr. Hamilton. I'm sure we will meet again."

This time Chad smiled. "Count on it."

CHAPTER TWENTY-SIX

"WHY DID you let us go to the other casino if you already knew that Strickland owned the Rio Cabuçu?" Ender asked.

"Because I wasn't one hundred percent sure, but I am now." Chad proceeded to tell Ender and Bo all that had happened at the Rio Cabuçu. Then he handed Ender the envelope, which had already been opened. "A little note from our long lost friend."

Ender opened the flap of the envelope and pulled out one single sheet of paper...

Dear Chad,

Let me be the first to welcome you to Rio de Janeiro! I hope your stay so far has been a delight. The beaches are incredible and the cuisine is amazing.

You and your little band of helpers have done a wonderful job. I thought it would take weeks for you to find me. You are everything I've ever wanted in a foe.

So, shall we say, Let The Games Begin!

Your friend,
Peter
PS. CATCH ME IF YOU CAN..........

ENDER HANDED the note and the envelope back to Chad. "Man, you've got to hand it to that guy, he's got style."

"That he does, Ender. It's going to be a real pleasure nailing him once and for all."

Kade said, "If he doesn't nail us first. Tell me something, Mr. Genius," he said looking straight at Chad. "Strickland has been one step ahead of us all the way and I can understand that because he always knows where we are. Is he really that good or is there someone in our inner circle that's feeding him information?"

Chad said, "My guess is both. He's definitely a criminal master-mind, with no conscience, *and* he has someone on the inside."

Mackenzie said, "But who?"

"Well let's see," as he looked around the room. "To be perfectly honest, I'd trust my life with anybody in this room," he paused. "With one exception."

The silence in the room was deafening as all eyes turned to Bo. He slowly glanced at each person: Chad, Mackenzie, Kade, Sydney, Ender, and Neal.

Bo smiled. "Wow, is this where I pull out my gun or just sit here and wet my pants?" He looked at Chad. "Have your director check me out and do whatever you want to satisfy yourself. I'm on your side and look forward to helping you get this guy Strickland, or Stevens, or whatever his name is."

Chad said. "I don't need to solicit the director's help on this. I've got Neal and he's better than anything the FBI can come up with." Ender nodded his head in agreement. "I had Neal check you out thoroughly and I'm happy to say you got the Neal Sweeny seal of approval, which is good enough for me."

"Here, here," Kade agreed.

Bo said, "I'm happy to be one of the team but that puts us back to square one. If it's not me and you trust everyone else here, where does that leave us?"

"Kade and I were kicking that around on the way to this meeting. I think he's onto something."

Bo looked Kade's way. "Remember the night we met when you thought you had the drop on us at the barracks?"

Bo said, "Uh, yeah. I'd like to forget about that. Not my finest moment."

"Well, if it makes you feel any better we knew you were coming and your reputation for the dramatic preceded you. I knew you'd try something cute so we were waiting in the shadows for you."

"That doesn't make me feel better, but go on."

"As I was saying, just before you got there we were trying to figure out how Peter found out so quickly we weren't in Thailand, that we had sent three agents who resembled us so it would buy us at least a couple of days in Seoul before we were discovered. It took only hours. That's another reason we were on our toes when you tried to sneak up on us."

"So you think that one of those agents might be the mole."

Chad said, "Maybe. Ender, why don't you call the director and have him look into it? Check out our pilots and anyone connected. Neal is already checking out all their finances to see if anyone has come into a large sum of cash. Have you had any luck yet?"

"No," Neal said. "But if it's there, I'll find it."

"I have no doubt," Chad smiled.

"Okay" Ender said, "Back to the casino. Chad I know you're a very, very smart man..."

"Not that smart," Kade interjected.

Everyone laughed except Chad who pretended to be hurt.

"Back to my question," Ender said. "You must've been counting cards but...."

"Good question," Chad said, "and in this case, the big ugly

gentleman over there," Chad nodded towards Kade, "is right. When it comes to math, I am definitely not a smart man." He paused for effect. "But Neal is. I had a special earpiece that Kade had in his little arsenal of CIA paraphernalia, which I'm sure Bo knows all about."

Bo nodded.

"The second button on my shirt was in reality a microphone and Mackenzie's pendant was a camera. So Neal was with us all the way. The plan was to get caught counting cards..."

"So you could get into the office and do some snooping. A little dangerous but I like it."

Mackenzie said, "A little dangerous?! I was beside myself! They wouldn't let me come with them when Chad was escorted into the office."

"Ah, Mac, everything worked out okay."

"Not like that time we were in Chad," Kade whispered.

Mackenzie said, "What? In Chad? What are you talking about?"

Kade said, "Oops. Sorry. Was that out loud?"

Mackenzie tilted her head at Kade.

"I meant the country of Chad, in Africa."

"Now would not be a good time for this Kade," Chad mumbled.

"Sure it would. Ease the tension in the room. As usual, we were on a rescue mission in some remote area of Chad, but we weren't quite sure where the prisoners were. So we devised a plan for Chad to get captured while I watched from the trees a hundred yards away with my rifle and scope. The plan was for Chad to stumble into the rebel camp by accident, get captured and locked up wherever they were hiding the prisoners. I was to watch and then follow to where the holding cell was."

"Did it work?" Sydney asked. "Seems like Chad was put into a treacherous position."

"It was a chance I was willing to take," Kade smiled.

"Didn't go too well for you either, did it, big shot?" Chad said sarcastically.

Kade winced. "Not exactly. Instead of taking Chad off to where the prisoners were being held, they dragged him into the nearest hut to interrogate the poor boy. I knew that wasn't good so I maneuvered around the camp in the jungle and got to the back of the hut."

Sydney said, "Obviously you got him out of there since you are both alive and well."

"*Au contraire,* Sydney," Chad lamented. "Kade was seen by one of the rebels and escorted into the hut to join me."

Bo said, "Uh oh, that doesn't sound good."

Chad said, "No, it wasn't. They beat us to a pulp."

"Yes, but the good news is, when they finished with what was left of us, they put us with the other prisoners to be executed the next morning."

"How did you get out?" Mackenzie asked,

"That's another long story we'll talk about later," Chad said. "The other good news is they broke Kade's jaw so I had a little peace and quiet for the next month."

Sydney put her arm around Kade. "My poor baby." Kade frowned and laid his head on Sydney's shoulder.

"So, Kade," Mackenzie said. "You brought up this story to make me feel better, did you?"

"Sorry, Mackenzie, I really thought I was talking to myself."

"Which he does a lot," Chad added as the others laughed.

"Okay, back to the business at hand. The bad news is that Peter Strickland knows we are here."

Ender said, "There's good news with that?"

"Yes," Chad said. "He won't know where we are anymore."

CHAPTER TWENTY-SEVEN

"I THINK he knows exactly where we are. But he won't after today. We will be on equal ground for the first time since we brought him down last year." Chad handed them all new phones. "These are burner phones. While we're here in Rio, you'll get a new phone every week. I've booked you all into different hotels in pairs, which we will also change each week if necessary. I'm hoping we can wrap this up soon. Bo has arranged for us all to have new identities, which are the names you are registered in at your new location. Your phone, thanks to Neal, has all the new phone numbers and here is a list of your new names and your new passports and IDs."

Sydney said, "Bo, how in the world did you get these ID's and so fast?"

Bo smiled, "I'd tell you but then...."

"I'd have to kill you," everyone chimed in unison.

Chad said, "All right, I'd suggest we all get a good night's sleep. We'll meet for breakfast tomorrow in the main floor restaurant and then we'll split up and go our separate ways. Right now, I'm sure there's only one set of trackers and they'll make a quick decision to follow me. Kade and I will have a big surprise for them. Starting tomorrow Mr. Paul Stevens aka Peter Strickland will begin being the hunted instead of the hunter."

"I like the sound of that," Ender said.

———

Well, Doug,

It's been a while since we last visited. What a run. I've been so busy with this Peter Strickland mess that we haven't talked baseball. Treat is doing an excellent job of getting the groundwork laid. Next week the city of Montreal is going to vote on the team name. I think the consensus is it's going to be the Expos. I can understand that. Can't wait to get back to my team and all the beautiful challenges that that entails. But for now it's all Strickland. I'm hoping to start turning the tables on him. While I was in his manager's office, I was able to capture the signal and GPS on his phone. Don't ask me how because I haven't got a clue. It's all Neal and his brilliant knowledge and use of technology. He even says he can hack the manager's laptop and install some kind of Trojan horse in it to get the location of Peter's laptop if they communicate that way. Can you believe that? Anyway, what all that means is we're getting close and are now sitting on equal ground. For now, we will be on the offensive and that feels good! While I was sitting across from the manager, I was able to attach a bug to the underside of his desk. We already know that he called Peter after I left, but he used the house phone so we don't have a location yet, but we will get it. It's only a matter of time until he uses his cell phone. Then we'll get a number, and hopefully a location. I'm sure it will be near the casino. The work starts tomorrow. Goodnight, Doug.

———

KADE TOOK A BIG BITE. "My, oh my, this omelet is to die for."

"The cuisine is good here, isn't it?" Chad said. "I'm definitely going to miss it. All right, to the business at hand. When we leave here the plan is to go off in all directions. I have rental cars all arranged for each of you. Sydney, you and Mac will rendezvous in a couple of hours after you've both settled into your new hotels. Sydney, you'll turn in your car and then you girls will stay together from then on. I've arranged for a two-bedroom suite at Mac's hotel so you won't even need to go back to your room. It's just to make it a little harder to track you down. Bo, you and Ender will do the same. Once you meet up later, I want you to stay together. That goes for everyone, except Neal. He's already on his way back to Boston. His devices are in place. The rest he can do from home."

He looked at Kade who was still enjoying his omelet. "That leaves you and me, buddy. We're going to leave here together to ensure that their little stakeout will follow us. We'll let them tail us for a while and then we'll turn the tables on them. That's when Peter will find out he's now on the defensive. He won't like that and I'm hoping he'll make a mistake trying to get control back. We're ready for everything he's got except one thing."

Mackenzie asked, "What's that?"

"The unknown," Kade said. "Nothing ever goes completely according to plan. If you're prepared then you just try to adapt."

Sydney said, "Are you boys any good at adapting?"

"Absolutely. That's when we're at our finest."

"Kade taught me a lot about reacting to sudden changes in a plan of action," Chad explained. "The biggest thing is not to panic and keep your wits about you."

Mackenzie said, "Or in the case of you two, your sense of humor."

"That has certainly got us through a few tight spots," Chad said.

"Like what?" Ender asked.

"Some other time, over drinks maybe. Let's concentrate on the business at hand."

Kade said, "And the business at hand is Peter Strickland."

"Exactly," Chad said. "This guy is, if nothing else, a real pro. Need I remind you that numerous people have died at his hands and that both Katie and my grandfather were almost part of that number?"

Everyone nodded but said nothing.

"Alright then, let's get going."

———

"There they are, over there," Chad indicated.

"I see them. What do you say, shall we go introduce ourselves?"

"Oh, I think they know who we are."

Kade said, "Just the same, I'd really like to get better acquainted."

"By all means, let's do it."

Chad and Kade put their luggage in the trunk of their rental and then headed straight for the two watchmen.

"How ya doin'?" Chad said loudly, extending his hand as they got closer.

The two said nothing.

Kade said, "Cat got your tongue, boys?"

At 6'1' and 6'3" respectively, Chad and Kade were pretty formidable, but nothing compared to these two behemoths. Like all of Strickland's bodyguards and cronies, they looked like they spent many hours daily at the gym and a little extra time getting their steroid injections.

"You don't know who you are dealing with, mister," said the apparent leader.

———

Chad looked at Kade. "You know that's the fourth time I've heard that statement from one of Peter's buddies. Three are dead and one is buried deep in the prison system where he will never see the light of day again."

"Some people just never learn," Kade said. "Just simply big and stupid."

Chad said. "Okay, gentlemen, here's what I know. You've been assigned by Strickland to keep an eye on us, am I correct so far?"

They said nothing. "Now I know for sure that nothing would give you more pleasure than to do what you were trained for and that's to beat us to a pulp and then put a bullet through our heads, right?"

The guy in charge smiled.

"I thought so. But you and I both know that that's not going to happen, is it? Peter has been planning my demise for months and if you spoil it, you two won't live through the night. So here's what's going to happen. Kade and I are going to get into our car and drive around for a while; don't worry, it will be nice and slow so you can keep up. Then after a time we are going to drive to some remote area, pull over and get out. If you are still with us then Kade and I are going to have to teach you two ladies some manners. I'd suggest while you're driving, that you," he pointed to the other guy, "call Peter and explain to him the situation. He'll either tell you to back off and pull away or to go ahead and engage us. You can't kill us but maybe you could put a whole lot of hurt on us. Now lastly, I have to warn you, Kade and I have never been beat when we're together. Peter knows that very well."

Chad let that sink in, saying nothing.

Kade said, "How about it, guys, you care to go for the championship?"

The lead guy smiled. "I'm going to love making you eat those words, both of you."

"Okay then, see you in a few!"

"WE'VE BEEN on the road now for about thirty minutes and they're still with us," Kade informed. "I don't know about you but I'm pretty well pumped."

"A little too confident aren't we, Mr. Kincaid? Those two looked like they could do some damage, and if I'm right, they're on steroids which means they have a very elevated pain threshold." Chad looked around. "I'm going to head towards the beach. Maybe we can find somewhere a little less crowded."

———

A FEW MINUTES LATER, with Peter's men still following them, Chad found a huge parking lot that led to the beach. It wasn't busy at all so he pulled over. The car that was following them also pulled over and stopped about fifty feet behind them. As Chad turned off the car he looked at Kade, who in turn was staring at Chad, grinning.

"You're enjoying this, aren't you? We aren't invincible, you know."

"Look Chadwick, if you have a headache you can stay in the car. I'll be back in a few."

Chad chuckled. "No, no, I'll go with you. Sorry to spoil your fun." He reached for the door handle. "Let's do it."

CHAPTER TWENTY-EIGHT

THEY WALKED towards Strickland's men who were already out of the car. They were both wearing polo shirts that showed off their bulging biceps, and a pair of beige chino pants. Chad was practically dressed the same, as was Kade, although Kade was wearing a pair of dark brown shorts.

Chad said, "I can't believe Peter is letting you guys do this."

"Actually," said the one, "I never called him. There's a lot I can do to you and still let you live to see another day." He looked at Kade. "You, on the other hand, don't have that type of protection. I'm personally going to punish you and at the end, just before I snap your neck, you'll be begging me to end it."

Kade shifted restlessly. "Okay, princess. We gave you every opportunity to back off. You'd think after all this time that Peter would realize you cavemen are no match for us. Oh wait, I forgot. You didn't call him, did you? Big mistake."

"Enough talk," the big guy said, as he started walking towards Kade, lifting his fists like a boxer. The second guy started towards Chad. Before the first one got to him, Kade took two steps forward, smashing the guy with a left hook and then a right that broke the man's nose. The big guy stopped, shook his head violently, wiped some of the blood from his face, tasted it, and then smiled at Kade as if to say *Is that all you got?*

"Uh oh," Kade mumbled under his breath as the man rushed him.

Meanwhile the other chap was circling Chad, sizing him up. Chad didn't like that. Men usually came right at him in an effort to get the first advantage, which was always to Chad's benefit. This guy was smarter, which told Chad immediately that he had his work cut out for him. So, Chad decided to go on the offensive. Forgetting his martial arts capability he, like Kade, took the first step forward and swung, aiming for the guy's jaw. The bad guy caught Chad's fist in the palm of his hand, smiled, and shoved Chad backward to the ground. A shocked Chad was sitting on his butt looking up at his assailant who, like his partner, was smiling. Chad looked over at Kade who was now being held in a bear hug, the air being squeezed right out of him. As if saying *having fun yet?* Chad grinned at Kade.

It was right then they both realized they might be in for the fight of their lives. These two were more fearsome than Duke's cronies from six months ago. That fight ended before it began, but this one was going to take some serious effort. Of the two of them, Chad was the better fighter in an organized gym fight, but on the street there was none better than Kade.

Pretending to be stuck in the bear hug, he relaxed and let his neck slump back, as if to be in the last throes of death, when he snapped his head forward, smashing into the man's already broken nose. He then brought his hands up in a flash, banging against the goon's ears, breaking both eardrums. As the guy released Kade to hold the sides of his own head, Kade stepped back and tucked his arm efficiently to his side, made a fist, and thrust it into the man's throat with all the force and power he had, shattering his windpipe. With no way to breathe, he slowly sank to the ground, sucking for air, but to no avail. He was dead within a minute. Kade stared down at the man for a moment and then glanced over to see how Chad was faring.

Chad's fight was completely different. It looked like a scene from a Chuck Norris movie. Both were getting in some brutal blows but the bigger man seemed to be a little too confident, enjoying the fight with a little smirk on his face. As Kade looked at Chad, he said to himself, "That's my boy." Chad had a cut lip that was going to need some stitches but Kade saw in his eyes that the other guy had no chance. Chad was totally focused. All of a sudden, instead of circling each other as they'd been doing, Chad leapt forward with both fists in the air, and brought them down like two hammers, smashing both of his foe's collar-bones, leaving him totally incapacitated. He stared at Chad and then, without thinking, came forward.

Chad stuck up one hand and screamed, "Stop!"

The man stopped.

"You have no chance. Look over at your partner. He's dead. Do you want to end up like him?"

The guy looked over at the still body.

"It's over. Here's what I see as your options: one, we take you to the hospital, get you the medical attention you need, and turn you over to the police. Then Peter Strickland will bail you out and you'll be dead within twenty-four hours. Peter doesn't accept failure. Two, we take you to the hospital, get you the medical attention you need, and then you disappear. I'm sure your partner has a cell phone with Peter's number on it but he never called him, his ego got in the way. Look what it got him. I'm sure you have some money put away. Get out of here and start a new life."

Chad paused. "Three."

The man looked surprised.

"Three, you can keep coming and we'll end this right now."

The man looked totally defeated. He looked over at his dead partner, put his head down and said nothing. Finally he spoke. "Two."

———

"WHAT'S YOUR NAME?" Chad asked.

"Giorgio."

"Well, Giorgio, if it's any consolation, you are one of the toughest guys I've ever fought. Six stitches in my lip and my body hurts so bad I'm not sure if I'll be able to move tomorrow." He held up the phone. "What was your partner's name?"

"Pau."

"How often does he call in?"

"Every night."

"Okay, it's three so we've got some time."

"Tell me, how does a guy like you get into this business? You certainly don't go to school for it."

"I don't know. I think most of us just drift that way. A fight here, a fight there; trouble with the cops, trouble with my father." Giorgio winced as he shifted positions. "Who knows? Then one day you're approached by a guy with a wad of bills wanting to know if you'd like some."

"Would you like out?"

"And do what? You make it sound so easy. This is all I know."

Chad said, "So your name is Giorgio. What is that? Italian? Are you from Italy?"

Giorgio nodded. "Yes, it's Italian. And no, I'm not from Italy. I'm from the Bronx."

"Shut up!" Kade said as he strolled into the ER cubicle.

Giorgio smiled.

"The cops are here," Kade said. "With some questions."

"Great!" an exasperated Chad said. He looked at Giorgio. "We're not done here. You just keep your mouth shut and you might get out of this, *capisce?*"

Giorgio nodded.

"Okay," Chad said to Kade. "Send them in."

"Mister Hamilton, my name is Lieutenant Gaspar."

"Please call me Chad, Lieutenant. Gaspar, that doesn't sound like a Brazilian name and your English is definitely not native."

"No, I'm from England originally but I've been here for over twenty years. So, Chad, would you like to tell me what's going on?"

"No, not really, Lieutenant," Chad smiled. "But what I'm about to tell you can be verified by your chief officer of the state of Rio de Janeiro, Manuel Huertas. We are part of a joint effort with the United States' FBI and CIA. That's all I can tell you about that. The rest you'll have to hear from Chief Huertas. What I can tell you is that the three of us were attacked by a group of men in that parking lot where you found the dead body. Isn't that right, Kade?" Chad went silent and then said, "Isn't that right, Kade?"

Kade almost choked on the Coke he was sipping on. His head snapped towards Chad, as did Giorgio's. *The three of us!*

"Er, uh, right, Lieutenant. They attacked the three of us."

"Why the dead body?"

"I'm afraid I did that," Kade said.

"When it was obvious that we were getting the drop on them, they jumped in their car and took off," Chad said.

The lieutenant said. "Then whose car is that, still sitting in the parking lot?"

"It's theirs. I guess with one of their men down they instinctively all jumped in the one car and took off."

Kade said nothing. *Good lord, Chad, you lie with the best of them!*

There was a deafening silence in the room. Finally the Lieutenant said. "Okay, gentlemen, that's all for now. I'll put in that call to Chief Huertas and we'll go from there." He walked out of the room.

Kade said, "Would you like to tell me what's going on? The *three* of us?" He pointed to Giorgio. "He nearly took your head off. You want to take a look in the mirror and see that swollen face of yours?"

Chad said nothing.

Giorgio said nothing.

Chad said, "Okay, Giorgio, the ball is in your court. Option four is this... I call Peter in a few minutes and let him know that you and Pau are dead. Then we put you up somewhere to let you heal. When we finish our business with Peter, and believe me, we will finish it, you come back with us to the States and we'll go from there." Chad paused for a moment. "What do you say?"

Giorgio sat still for what seemed like an eternity. Then he said, "Why would you do that for me? I don't understand. I've never met anybody like you!"

"And you never will again, Giorgio," said Kade. "Trust me and take the deal."

More silence. Finally Giorgio nodded and said, "Okay, I'll give it a try." Then he sat silent again and finally, without looking up said, "Thanks."

CHAPTER TWENTY-NINE

"Chad, you realize you can't save the world, don't you?" Kade asked.

"I do know that, Kade. I'm not a saint or anything close to it. But I made a commitment long ago that what I could do, I would do."

"A commitment to whom?"

"I don't know, to myself I suppose. I can't explain it. I just know I'm compelled to do it."

Kade said, "Okay. Just know that I'll always have your back because I was the first one you saved."

Chad stared at Kade and finally said, "Is this where we hug?"

"Come near me and you'll end up with some more stitches in that lip of yours. By the way, good luck explaining Giorgio to Mackenzie."

"I've been thinking about that," Chad lamented.

———

"How can you possibly trust him?"

"Ah, Mac. Let me ask you a question. Do you trust me?"

"With my life. It's your judgment that sometimes scares me. You seem to look at others through those rose-colored glasses of yours. This guy Giorgio tried to beat you up. What makes you think he won't come after you again, first chance he gets?"

"I don't know," Chad said. "That's why I set up some safeguards until I am sure. He gave us some valuable information regarding Strickland."

"Like what?"

"He knows that Peter has an escape plan if things go south. Peter is aware that the United States and Brazil have an extradition agreement."

"Can't you go to the police and let them know what's going on?" Mackenzie asked.

"Not yet. The reputation of the police in Brazil is less than stellar. Over sixty percent of the population doesn't trust the police. But with the backing of the FBI Director and the CIA, we have other very reliable help. Right now, Ender and Bo are staking out the casino and checking the perimeter for any escape options. I'm hoping that they come up with something soon."

———

"HAVE YOU BEEN ON MANY STAKEOUTS?" Ender asked as he took a bite out of his sandwich.

Bo said, "Are you kidding? Seems like I've spent most of my time on these types of assignments. I call it 'hurry up and wait.' At times I've been a spotter for sharpshooters like Kade. In some cases we've laid on our stomachs for hours waiting for the right opportunity to get the job done."

"I hear you. Last year my partner and I spent nearly ten days in an abandoned apartment across the street from a suspected terrorist before we got the info we needed to nail him. You know, we've been sitting here for several hours waiting for who knows what. What do you say we take a walk and see if we can find any suspicious-looking buildings? If Chad's right and there are some tunnels leading out of the casino to safety, maybe we can spot one of them."

"We'd have to be pretty lucky but I believe in luck and I could use some physical activity. Let's do it."

Bo and Ender were parked on a side road just east of the casino. The casino itself was nestled against a sandy beach with a breathtaking view of the ocean, so they started on the beach and began strolling inland. Both were clad in shorts and linen button-down shirts that made them look like a couple of vacationers taking in the scenery.

"I could definitely get used to this."

"Yeah," Bo said. "Maybe if and when we nail Strickland, we can stay for a little R&R. But I doubt it. Usually on to the next assignment."

"No *ifs* about finding Peter. Chad isn't about to let this go. It's really gotten personal."

"How so?" Bo asked. "I really wasn't filled in on the whole story. For me it all happened pretty fast. I was in Thailand, then abruptly told that it had changed to Seoul, and then before I could say *hello* we found ourselves in the brig à la General Markum and his band of merry men."

Ender chuckled to himself as they continued on their walk. "As you know, Chad likes to find companies on the selling block, but instead of being the typical corporate raider, he tries to do what's best for all involved. This all got started about eight months ago with Evans Pharmaceuticals."

"Isn't that Mackenzie's last name?"

"It is." Ender proceeded to explain the whole situation, including the kidnapping of Chad's twin sister, Katie, the near miss at his grandfather's wedding, the death of the Sandersons on their boat, and all the other deaths and happenings at the hands of Peter Strickland.

"Man, he sounds like a real piece of work. And it sounds like your FBI compadres screwed up at the courthouse when Strickland escaped."

"Not our finest moment. But you can see why Chad has made this so personal. He won't rest until he's nailed him!"

"Okay, but Chad's a civilian. Yet he seems to be in charge."

"Trust me," Ender said. "He is in charge. The Director recruited him after seeing him in action. Then he tested Chad."

"How so?"

"He told Chad to back off or he would use all the resources the FBI had to silence him."

Bo said, "I take it things didn't work out too well for the Director."

"That's putting it mildly. Chad and his little crew, turned the tables on him, which is what the Director was hoping for."

"So Director Martelli liked what he saw?"

"That's putting it mildly. Chad was one of the best leaders the Special Forces ever had. In Kade he has one of the best the CIA ever had."

"I know all about Kade," Bo said. "His reputation as an assassin is without equal."

Ender said, "And then there's Neal; the best I or anyone in the FBI has ever seen with the computer. Together, the three of them make one nearly perfect super hero of the rarest sort. Chad intends to end this, right here, permanently. And he has the backing at the highest levels of the intelligence community. And of course, he can cheat. He doesn't have to follow the rules. Chad's the sort of a guy that won't abuse those powers but he'll do whatever is necessary to get the bad guy."

"No strings attached."

"Well, yes, there's one big catch. Even though the Director recruited Chad and knows all about this operation, if Chad gets caught, he's on his own. The FBI and all other official agencies will deny any knowledge of Chad and his players; so, needless to say, Chad intends to see this to the end. As far as he is concerned, either he or Peter Strickland is going down right here in Rio."

"You mean it ends right here with Peter's demise?"

Ender sighed. "Yep. Chad's the ultimate good guy. He didn't look for this, but because he and his family are the targets of this ruthless guy who has no conscience, Chad is going to make sure it ends here." Ender slowed his walk. "As long as we can find him."

Bo turned to look in the direction of Ender's gaze. "That's interesting."

"Isn't it?" Ender said. "All these nice villas and buildings and then we see this odd looking outcrop of a building. The average eye wouldn't even notice unless, like us, you were looking for it."

What they saw was a little grey building that looked like it might be some cover for a small utility shed.

"Let's check it out." As they got closer they noticed a padlock on the door.

"Hmmm," Ender mused.

"Ordinarily," Bo said, "That would be a problem."

"But you are no ordinary guy."

"Correctamundo, my friend." Bo pulled out a set of keys and a couple different lock picks. "This one ought to do it," he said as he fiddled with the lock. After only three seconds the lock opened.

Bo gave a big smile to Ender, who reciprocated.

They went inside to see nothing out of place or unusual. "Nothing much here," Bo said.

"Exactly, so why the lock?"

"Maybe to keep kids out."

"Yes, but why? This whole area is high class and beautiful," Ender said. "I thought maybe it was some kind of utility outbuilding or something. Nothing here but this old trash can in the corner." He kicked at it, moving it a foot or so. Underneath was more dirt but at one of the edges there was an infringement that looked out of place. Ender bent down to brush the dirt away. As the dirt was being removed there was some kind of object or flap beginning to appear. Both men looked at each other and again smiled with anticipation.

"Bingo," Bo said.

When the dirt was completely removed it appeared to be a trap door but had no way to open it. "That's interesting. No latch or notch or any way to pull it open."

Ender said, "Not if you only wanted it to open from the other side."

"Well let's see if we can't ..."

"Freeze!" the man said with his Uzi pointed at them.

CHAPTER THIRTY

"THAT LOOKS AWFUL." Mackenzie said referring to Chad's lip as she gently touched it. They were sitting on the couch in the living room of Chad's suite. "Does it hurt much?"

"Only when I laugh," he said sarcastically. "I'm okay, Mac. Nothing that won't heal."

She inched closer to him and tenderly kissed his lip at the point of the stitches. "Does that help the pain?"

Chad smiled, "What pain?"

"Any other spots that are hurting that I can be of assistance."

Chad was dressed in a pair of shorts and a light blue T-shirt. He pointed to a spot on his neck. "There."

Mackenzie kissed it affectionately.

He then lowered his hand to a spot just above his right peck and touched it without saying a word.

Mackenzie lovingly reached down tugging at the bottom of Chad's shirt and carefully pulled it up over his head, and then kissed the spot Chad had touched. She couldn't help but notice two more bruises, one on his shoulder and the other on his left arm.

"My goodness, Mr. Hamilton, what did this guy do to you?"

"Nothing I couldn't handle, Mac. Now where were we?"

A few minutes later Mackenzie said, "Oh Chad, I'm so scared. When is this going to end?"

Chad put his arms around Mackenzie and pulled her close. "Soon Mac, I promise."

"Is this even a promise you can keep? Strickland and his men are so dangerous. There seems to be no limit as to what he can do."

"We're close. I should be hearing from Ender and Bo any time now. Hopefully they'll have some good news for me."

———

"I'LL ASK you two just once more," the man with the Uzi said. "Who are you and what are you doing here."

"Where?" Bo asked, playing the dumb one. Ender picked up on it.

"Please don't hurt us. We are tourists here on vacation. We were just out for a walk and got curious. We mean no harm."

Bo said, "We saw this shack out here in the middle of this gorgeous area and decided to see what was inside."

"The door was padlocked," the man, who was in some kind of security uniform, said.

"What padlock? Honest sir, the door was standing wide open so we just walked in. As you can see, there's nothing in here to even be interested in. If it's okay with you, we will just be on our way." They both started for the door.

"Hold it right there," the guard said, shoving his gun up against Bo's chest.

Bo and Ender said nothing as the guard also stood silently contemplating his next move. Finally, after what seemed an eternity, he said, "If I ever catch you two anywhere near this place or anywhere in the area again, I'll shoot first and then if there's anything left of you, ask questions. You got that?"

Both said, "Yes, sir," as Ender reached out to hug the guy.

"Get outta here, now!"

As the two were jogging away from their little escapade, Bo said, "You little devil. I'm going to nominate you for an academy award."

———

"We didn't get to open the obvious hatch but I'd be willing to bet a month of Bo's salary that it was definitely going to be a tunnel that leads back to the casino," Ender said.

Bo laughed. "My salary, huh? But you are right. It's got to be an escape route."

Chad said, "Most likely not the only one, but it's a start. Nice work, guys. We're getting close. I think it's time we upped the pressure on Mr. Strickland." He reached for the phone he had confiscated earlier in the day and hit redial.

"It's about time you called in, I don't like people that are late," the voice said.

"So sorry, Peter. Pau asks me to send his regrets. He wasn't feeling well and is taking a nap, in the morgue."

Peter Strickland always exuded an air of confidence but Chad's voice on the other end of the line gave him pause. But only for a moment. "Chad, Chad, Chad, you continue to amaze me. What am I going to do with you?"

"How about we meet face to face and discuss it, Peter? This is between you and me so let's end it. Are you up to it? Come on, Peter. It's time to man up. With Pau and Giorgio dead, you keep losing men at an alarming rate. Eventually it's going to end up with just the two of us anyway, so, what do you say?"

"Your offer is tempting, Chad. A fight to the end. But this is my turf and I hold all the cards. You haven't suffered enough but we are getting close. Keep Pau's phone and we'll keep in touch."

"You mean the phone with the GPS? Nice try, Peter. One last thing. Get all your men together and whatever else it is that you think you can use against me and do it fast. I'm coming for you."

Chad hung up the phone, dropped it on the floor and smashed it with his heal. Picking up the remains he handed them to Ender. "Would you boys kindly drop this in a dumpster on your way back to your hotel? I'd appreciate it."

———

I have to admit it, Chad, you are amazing, which makes killing you all the better. But I think it's time to move up the schedule and go to plan B. I've never had a foe quite like you. I wish we could continue but it's like you said, I'm running out of good men. And you are the one who ruined all my grandiose plans in Boston and the years of planning that went into it. But before I end your life I'm going to see to it that your pain and suffering will have you begging for death.

———

"THIS PLACE IS ALMOST as good as Luigi's," Kade said as he sipped on his glass of Chardonnay. Luigi's was the Italian restaurant at Hamilton Towers.

Chad nodded. "I agree, although I'm not sure Luigi would agree."

Sydney said, "Well that's what makes Luigi the best. He holds himself to a higher standard."

Mackenzie smiled. "This is a lovely restaurant. It's relaxing after the day we've had, particularly you two," she said, looking at Chad and Kade. "I wonder where Ender and Bo are?"

"I don't know," Chad said, a little bit anxiously. "They said they saw another building on the other side of the casino that looked a little suspicious. They wanted to check it out after dark, hoping not to run into their friendly guard again. They should've been here by now. I hope they didn't encounter trouble again."

As if on cue, Bo and Ender came strolling in.

Kade said, "We were just discussing you two, wondering if you'd lost your way. How did it go?"

"First things first," Ender said. "I'm starving."

Chad laughed as he signaled for their waiter. "These two gentlemen say they're hungry enough to eat a horse. Can you accommodate them?"

"Afraid not," the waiter said with a wink. "But we have a filet mignon to die for."

"Sounds great," Ender said. "I'll have it medium rare smothered in sautéed mushrooms and your seasoned green beans."

Bo looked around the table, stopping at Sydney. He pointed to her plate. "That looks outstanding. Bring me that."

"Yes, sir," the waiter said. "Penne pasta with sausage marinara." He got the rest of his order and left to take care of it.

"Okay," Chad said, "now tell us what you found."

"Absolutely nothing." Ender said. "The reason we are so late is because that pesky guard caught us snooping around. He's actually pretty good. Even though we were watching out this time, he still got the drop on us. Not our finest hour."

"Well the fact that you're here talking to us means you got out of it," Kade said.

"Yeah, we disarmed him, tied him up, and took him to a location where he won't be found for a few hours."

Bo said, "But our cover is blown."

"That's okay," Chad said. "After my conversation with Strickland a while ago, he will be accelerating his plans."

"What makes you think so?" Sydney asked.

"Because that's what I would do. We are closing in and he knows it. His ego is too big to go into hiding. I think he wants to end this as bad as we do."

"What's our next move?" Kade asked.

"To enjoy our evening! I, for one, need to clear my head, as do the rest of you. And besides, Kade and I need to do a little healing too." He touched the stitches in his lip. "This is killing me. It hurts to chew."

Kade said as he rolled his shoulders, "Amen to that. That Pau fellow had the upper hand on me for a while. My whole body aches."

Mackenzie shook her head, "Yes, and you two loved every minute of it, didn't you?"

Chad glanced at Kade, both with somber looks on their faces. Chad cracked first, then they both burst into laughter.

"Guilty," Kade said.

"You two are psychological pygmies. Some day you are going to meet your match and then what are Mackenzie and I going to do?"

"Don't worry, Syd, you two gorgeous ladies would have no problem finding someone," Kade said. "Granted, not nearly as good-looking as Chad and me."

He screamed out as Sydney's perfectly placed toe found his shin.

"You didn't let me finish. You can relax because Chad and I will never meet our match!"

Bo caught Ender's surreptitious glance and both smiled at Kade's arrogance.

Chad sat back in his chair. "All I ever wanted was to have my little baseball team."

CHAPTER THIRTY-ONE

"THAT WAS one of the best meals I've ever had," Mackenzie said. "Don't tell Luigi, Chad."

"I won't. I think it tasted better because we were able to relax and enjoy ourselves. We'll give Luigi a chance to show his stuff when we get back. Dinner will be on me."

Kade smiled. "Need I remind you that this dinner is on you?"

Chad moaned, "Right. You are an expensive lot, aren't you? Let's go back to our respective hotels, continue to clear our heads, and get a good night's sleep. We'll meet in the morning at my hotel for breakfast with hopefully our final plans to get this guy. Ender, would you talk to the director and see if there is someone he knows in law enforcement, here in Rio, that can be completely trusted? I imagine we're going to need backup and all the help we can get."

"Will do, boss," Ender said. "Anyone up for a little late night racquetball?"

Both Chad and Kade moaned.

Kade said, "I can barely lift my arm."

Chad said, "There isn't any spot on my body that doesn't hurt."

"Exactly," Ender smiled. "My big chance for revenge."

"Tell you what, mister," Chad said. "Help us get Strickland and you can beat me anytime you want."

"That's what you said over six months ago, the first time we got him. Instead, you just didn't beat me quite as bad as usual."

Mackenzie laughed. "Face it, Ender. Chad's just too competitive when it comes to sports."

"Tell you what, Ender. When we get back to the States, I'll play you left-handed."

Ender said, "Not on your life. You'd most likely beat me and then I'd be humiliated. Let's just pretend this conversation never happened."

"Good idea," Kade said.

———

Back at Chad's room, he and Kade were going over a few scenarios.

"What do you think? Tomorrow the big showdown?"

Chad sighed. "I hope so. I'm growing weary of this mess. Mac thinks you and I are having a great time and she'd be right if it wasn't so personal. We've got to get this guy now."

"We will, pal, I promise."

Chad's phone rang. He looked at the display and smiled. "Couldn't get enough of me tonight, huh, Mac?"

"Chad." Her voice was quivering.

Chad felt his stomach jump.

"What's wrong, Mackenzie?"

A man's voice answered. "Nothing, as long as you do what you're told."

"Who is this?" Chad demanded.

"You don't ask the questions, Hamilton, I do. Now listen carefully. I have a message from Peter Strickland."

Chad said nothing.

"Nothing is going to happen to your girlfriend. Mr. Strickland just wanted your attention. Do I have it?"

Again Chad said nothing. The wheels in his head were already working. Kade jumped to his feet when he realized what was happening.

"Like you, he wants to end this, so listen up. You and your little buddy, be ready to move tomorrow by 6 am. You'll be getting a call with further instructions then."

"Let me talk to Mackenzie."

The phone clicked off.

Chad sat silently for a moment then looked up at Kade. "Tomorrow morning I'll get a call. You've been invited to the party."

"Good. So they have Mackenzie and Syd?"

Chad looked at Kade and shook his head. "They didn't say anything about Sydney."

Kade's eyes grew wide.

Chad dialed Mackenzie and Sydney's hotel. After the receptionist answered, Chad asked, "Has anything abnormal or alarming happened tonight?"

"Why, yes," the operator said. "As a matter of fact, something has."

Chad tried to remain calm. "And what would that be?"

"Some guests saw a woman being forced into a minivan that then drove away with her in it."

"Did anyone get a license number or a description?"

"Well, the police were here but you'd have to check with them. With all the commotion it's hard to say. We've never had anything like this happen before. Imagine a kidnapping and shooting all on the same night."

"What shooting?" Chad asked unsteadily.

"The other woman. One was apparently kidnapped and the other was shot."

CHAPTER THIRTY-TWO

KADE BURST through the emergency room doors, heading straight for the front desk.

"Sydney Nichols. Where is she?" he demanded, but it sounded more like pleading.

The receptionist said in an experienced kindly voice. "Are you a relative?"

Kade knew the routine. "Yes, I'm her husband. Where is she?" he said even louder than the first time.

"Just a moment, sir, and I'll get the attending doctor."

"Can't you just answer the question, please?"

"I'm sorry, Mr...?"

"Kincaid, Jake Kincaid."

"I'm sorry, Mr. Kincaid. I honestly don't know. Let me get Dr. Toliver." She picked up the phone and pressed a button. "Would you please ask Dr. Toliver to come to the front desk?" She hung up the phone. "He'll be right with you."

Chad put his hand on Kade's shoulder and thanked the lady. "Come on buddy, we should know something in just a minute."

Dr. Toliver came walking through the double swinging doors

looking at the receptionist who in turn pointed to Kade. He walked up and extended his hand. "I'm Dr. Toliver. You're Sydney Nichols' husband?"

"Yes, how is she?" a now frantic Kade asked.

"She is in surgery."

"Surgery? What's wrong? Is she going to be okay?"

"The surgery is fairly normal. She was shot in the upper right chest and shoulder. It shattered her collarbone so they need to put some pins in it. The danger is that she lost a lot of blood, but she is young and looks like she's in good shape. There is always danger from the trauma of a gunshot wound and loss of blood but I think she is going to be okay. Surgery should be over in less than an hour."

"Will I be able to see her?"

"Yes, of course. She's going to be very weak. This nurse will take you up to the surgical waiting room."

"Thank you, doctor," Chad said. "You've been very helpful."

———

"No way this guy lives," Kade said.

"I know. I told the Director that we'd catch him and they could extradite him back to the United States. He assured me that the FBI has ways of putting someone away permanently and that Strickland would never see the light of day for the rest of his miserable life."

"But that's not going to happen, is it Chad?" Kade had a hardened look on his face, as did Chad.

"No, it's not. Peter Strickland will never see the USA again, I promise."

———

"Hey," a groggy Sydney said as she looked up at Kade.

"Hey, yourself," Kade said through moist eyes. "How ya feelin'?"

"Like I've been shot," she mumbled. "Where's Mackenzie?"

Chad said, "Don't worry about Mackenzie. You just get some rest."

A tear fell down the side of Sydney's face. "They've got her, don't they?"

"They do," Kade said. "But don't you worry your pretty little face. Chad and I are getting her back soon, and then we can all go home."

Sydney sighed, "You be careful, Michael. I've put a lot of time into you." She smiled weakly as she closed her eyes.

"You gentlemen will have to leave now."

"Thank you, nurse," Chad said. "Please take good care of her."

———

"Every time I drop my guard, even for a minute, Strickland makes a move. I should have known by now," Chad said as they were driving back to the hotel.

Kade said. "We have about six hours. Let's make good use of them."

"Right. Bo and Ender are meeting us. We've got lots of work to do."

"You know that Peter is not going to give you Mackenzie just like that."

"I know. It's all about making me suffer right up to the end. I think that's why he's allowing you to come."

"Fine with me," Kade said. "I told you that you get first shot at him. I'll keep that promise. But after what he did to Syd and Mackenzie, there's no way he lives."

"I agree, but first of all we've got one minor problem."

"You mean the trap that we'll be walking into?"

"Yep. The four of us have got to put our heads together, come up with some scenarios and then find some solutions." As Chad was pulling into the garage he spotted Bo and Ender. "There they are. Let's go up to the penthouse and get to it."

As they were heading for Chad's room, Bo said, "Do you think they'll run you two all over the place before they get you to Macken-zie's location?"

Chad said, "No, I think they'll disarm us and take us there. They know we are too smart for games. I'll be hooked up so I can communi-cate to you where we are at first. Then I'm sure they'll find the device and remove it. When they transport us to wherever we're going, you'll have to follow us," he said to Bo. "Ender, by then you'll be in the vicinity in your own car. Bo will communicate with you, so that you can take over the pursuit; hopefully keep them from spotting you. We're going to put a small GPS device in Kade's belt buckle. If they don't discover it, you won't need to have a visual on them and can follow from a distance."

"That should work," Ender said. "The real problem is when you arrive at the final destination."

Kade said, "We'll be ready. I don't care what they throw at us. Peter Strickland is going down."

"Okay," Chad said. "Let's go over some ideas. We need to ask ourselves what we would do and get prepared. We'll use Bo's car and load it up with the supplies that we may need."

"Be a good idea to do the same with my car too," Ender said. "Just in case something goes wrong with Bo."

"Nothing is going to go wrong with me," Bo interjected.

"It is a good idea," Chad said. "Can't be too careful. Look at all the curves Strickland has thrown at us so far." Bo nodded. "Okay, let's get to it. Kade, what would you do if you had kidnapped Mackenzie?"

They spent the next hour and a half going through six different scenarios and how to get out of them. With two CIA operatives, one FBI agent, and Chad, they came up with some creative ideas and how to get around them. Now it was time to wait until six.

———

MACKENZIE SAT in a room with no windows and one light fixture above her on the ceiling. She had been blindfolded so she had no idea where they had taken her. After they had removed her from the car, she felt a concrete type floor and heard some echoes when doors were opened and closed. She sensed that they were in or near some kind of warehouses. She was terrified as she sat still on the edge of a metal chair.

Oh, Chad! What are we going to do? Seems like all I've brought you is trouble. Do I wish that we had never met? Sometimes I think it would be better if we hadn't. But you've become the love of my life and I yours. I can't imagine my life without you. Are we ever going to find peace or will Peter Strickland win and destroy us. What are you thinking at this moment? You must be as terrified as I am. And what of Sydney? All I saw was her lying in a pool of blood as they whisked me away. Kade must be beside himself. Will this ever end? Chad, I'm so scared. Will you be my hero and save the day? Actually, you're already my hero. Please be careful but come and get me!

———

"CHAD, so nice to hear your voice. I hope you boys had a lovely evening?"

"Cut the crap, Peter, and get on with it."

"Oh you sound so tense. Might I suggest a great masseuse? She'll do wonders for you."

Chad said nothing.

"Okay, Chad," Peter sighed. "Why don't you and Kade meet some of my associates at the front of my casino? Fifteen minutes."

The phone clicked off.

Chad looked at the other guys. "Are we ready?"

"Let's do it," Kade said. "It's our turn to win, permanently."

CHAPTER THIRTY-THREE

As CHAD and Kade drove into the casino's parking lot, they saw three large guys wearing jeans and polo shirts at the front of the entrance.

"There's our welcoming party."

"Rather impressive looking, aren't they?" Kade said.

Chad casually asked, "Can you hear me, boys?"

"Affirmative," Bo said.

"Loud and clear," was Ender's reply.

"Okay then," Chad said. "Here we go."

———

CHAD AND KADE were escorted into the manager's office. Chad had been there once before so he was familiar with its surroundings. They were relieved of their guns and Chad's listening device was easily discovered, as Chad knew it would be. Since Peter at the moment was holding all the cards, including Mackenzie, he figured they would be put through the normal search, but nothing more. He was right. The GPS on Kade's belt buckle went undetected. Good news!

"So, where are we headed?" Chad asked.

The man who seemed to be in charge smiled, as if to say, *really?*

Chad continued, "I know you can hear me Peter. You know how this is going to end; it's either you or me. Why don't we stop all these charades? Let's skip all this playing around. Just the two of us; best man wins."

The room went silent.

Finally Chad heard a clicking sound. "Nice try, Chad, but we already know who the best man is. Before I take permanent care of you, I'm going to make you pay for the pain that you've caused me. I had it all: fame, prestige, all the trappings of success, and much, much more. You took some of it away, which I no doubt will get back, but first I will eliminate the thorn in my side, you. By the way, after you're dead, I'm going to continue to ruin everyone and everything that's dear to you. The name Chad Hamilton will be ruined and anyone connected to you will rue the day they were ever born."

"Talk's cheap, Strickland. Let's get to it," Chad said.

"You're so right, Chad. See you in a few."

Chad and Kade were blindfolded and led to a car behind the casino. Chad assumed that the third button on his shirt, a microphone to Bo and Ender, was still working. "Where are we headed boys? Maybe I can show you a shortcut."

"Thanks, Hamilton," the one in charge said sarcastically, "but I'll manage."

"You know," Kade said, "just about anyone that's been connected with Peter has been eliminated by Chad and me. I'd be a little concerned if I were you two."

"Oh, you might be able to take us, which I doubt, but then you'd never see that girlfriend of Hamilton's alive. I don't think you'll do anything to ruin that. Peter said you two are pretty smart. Maybe when this is all over and if, and it's a big if, we will get a chance to go at each other, we'll see who the better men are."

Chad said, "We already know who that is, junior. In fact, I'm looking forward to getting to know you better."

The man Chad called junior, threw his head back and laughed. He knew of Chad and Kade's skills, but he also knew that Chad, Kade, and Mackenzie would all be dead within the hour.

———

AFTER ABOUT AN HOUR OF RIDING, Chad said, "So we've gone over the same tracks twice now. If you guys have any idea what you're doing you know by now that no one is following you. So let's get to it, boys. Take us to Mackenzie and Peter."

"As a matter of fact, we are arriving as we speak." The car came to a stop. "You two may get out now. If you take off your blindfolds you'll see that there are now six of us with fully loaded guns pointed at you. I don't care how good you think you two are, six against two is impossible."

Kade smiled. "Normally I'd say six against us is just about right, but your guns may give you a slight advantage."

There was a row of warehouses along a dock about fifty feet from the water. Chad could see that the only way in was from the road that they had come on. The bad news is that it was also the only way out. He and Kade made mental notes of the surrounding area and looked at each other. Advantage Peter Strickland. They were led to the fourth warehouse and led through a metal door, which entered a hallway. The hallway curved slightly and then entered into the main area. At the far right was a large steel desk as was the case on the far left. What he saw in the middle, fifty feet away, nearly stopped his heart. Mackenzie was strapped to a metal chair. Two more chairs were on either side of her, about five feet away. Chad and Kade were led to the chairs and strapped to each one. Their legs were attached to the legs of the chairs and their hands were tied behind their backs. Then their captors left, leaving the three in their chairs.

Chad looked at Mackenzie and smiled. "How are you, Mac?"

She managed a small but feeble smile. "I've been better. It's good to see you two." She looked at Kade. "I saw them shoot Sydney. I'm so sorry."

"It's okay, Mackenzie. She made it through surgery and is going to pull through. Don't worry, you'll see her again."

"Oh, I wouldn't count on that Mackenzie," Peter Strickland said as he came walking in, followed by three of his gunmen. "Chad, we finally meet face to face after all this time. It's been way too long."

"Tell me, Peter," Chad said. "How does a piece of garbage like you live with himself?"

"Quite well, thank you. You see, Chad, there are givers and takers in this world. Now you, my friend, are a giver and that is admirable. I, on the other hand, am a taker and a giver. I take what I want and once in a while I like to give. But mostly I take."

"I understand your warped code of conduct, Peter. If anyone gets in the way of your plans or success, too bad for them. But what about the Sandersons? You had them viciously murdered in front of their daughter. For what purpose?"

"Ah, the Sandersons, yes; but you see, Chad, I did have a purpose behind that. It was to get your attention. Did I, Chad?"

Kade interjected, "You are sick, Strickland. I promised Chad that he could personally take care of you but that's a promise I may not be able to keep."

"My my, do I need to remind you two that you are the ones who are tied up and I'm holding all the cards?"

Chad said, "We'll see who's holding all the cards in the end!"

"But you see, dear boy, this is the end. I'm tired of this cat and mouse game we have been playing. It's time for you to pay the piper. And before I take my leave, let me remind you of my promise. Even though you three will be dead minutes from now, I'm going to see that the rest of your family pays for your sins." He looked at Kade. "Starting with your detective lady friend. She'll never leave the hospital alive."

Kade had hate in his eyes as he spoke. "Sorry, Chad, I'm afraid I'm not going to be able to keep my promise. Strickland is mine."

"Tell you what, Kade," Chad said, "once we get out of here we'll bring this dirtbag down together; deal?"

"Deal."

Peter Strickland threw his head back as he exhibited a deep belly laugh. "You two are a real kick. I'm truly going to miss our time together. Mackenzie, I'm very sorry it has to end like this. It's been a pleasure." He half bowed to her as he turned and headed for the hallway entrance. "I know you two are amazing and no doubt can get out of those chairs, but I need to let you in on a secret. One of you three is sitting on a pressurized bomb. The minute you release any of your weight, boom, you're all dead. You have fifteen minutes to make peace with each other."

CHAPTER THIRTY-FOUR

STRICKLAND PULLED out what looked like a remote control. "Time starts now." With his back to them as he continued for the exit, he held the remote above his head so that they could see it, and pressed a button.

Chad yelled, "See you soon, Peter!"

Strickland ignored him and walked out.

———

KADE LOOKED OVER AT CHAD. "Well, Maestro, in all our planning last night I don't remember a scenario where we'd be sitting on a bomb."

"Oh, Chad, I'm so sorry." Mackenzie said.

"Don't start, Mac. We've been over this before. Helping to save your dad's company was the right thing to do. Need I point out to you *again* that as a result I now have you in my life? If things were to end right now, these past few months will have made it all worth it."

Mackenzie smiled weakly.

Kade said, "So which one of us is sitting on the bomb?"

"Not me," Chad said. "Peter wants me to suffer as long as possible. He knows that even if I got out of this chair there's nothing I could do about the bomb."

"That's a pretty weak theory but I think you're probably right. Then what?"

"I have a plan, but first let's get me out of here."

———

Nothing ever surprised Peter Strickland. He was ruthless and cunning and had been through just about every situation that life could throw at him. But he had to admit that this one stunned him. As he walked past the last warehouse someone grabbed his arm while a gun was pressed against his temple.

"Freeze Strickland," Bo said. "Give me the remote very carefully."

Strickland kept his composure and even smiled. "This remote won't help Hamilton and his friends. Once the bomb was activated even I can't stop it. They're as good as dead."

Bo and Ender had notified the police when they were sure of the location. They had already arrested three of Strickland's men and were waiting for Peter and his other three men when they came out of the warehouse. After turning Peter and his men over to the police, they sprinted for the warehouse that held their friends.

They entered the warehouse, raced down the hallway and into the main room. Chad was kneeling and looking under Mackenzie's chair.

"Good to see you, boys," Kade said calmly. "What took you so long?"

Chad looked up at Bo and Ender. "The bomb's here under Mackenzie. Get Kade loose fast. We've got nine minutes to work this out."

Chad looked at Ender. "Strickland?"

"We got him." Ender said grinning. "He's in police custody."

Kade said, "Not good enough, but we'll tackle that situation later. Did you get the remote?"

"Yes," said Bo. "But it's no help. We've checked it out. It was only there to start the bomb's countdown. We can't stop it."

———

"CHAD, you all need to get out of here before it's too late. I know you think this isn't my fault and I love you for it. But it's time to save yourselves and take care of Peter Strickland once and for all."

Chad took Mackenzie's face in his hands. "Please do me a favor and shut up." He smiled at her and tenderly kissed her. "We've been in much worse situations than this, haven't we, Kade?"

Kade stared at Chad for a second and then smiled. "Sure."

Chad said, "Ender, go to the cars and get all the vests you can find. Then check the police cars for any helmets and bring them all back here. And try and find some cotton. You have four minutes. GO!"

Ender darted for the hallway and disappeared.

"What now, Cupcake?" Kade knew that Chad seemed to be at his best under intense pressure. This was about as intense as it gets.

Chad pointed to the steel desk at the side of the room. "Bo, you and Kade bring that desk over here." As they proceeded to the desk, Chad took the straps off of Mackenzie's arms and legs. "Everything's going to be okay, Mac."

"Promise?"

"As always."

Mackenzie said, "If we get...."

Chad frowned at her.

"Okay, okay! *When* we get out of here, I think you should let Sydney and me take care of Peter!"

"Whoa," Kade said. "I almost feel sorry for him."

Ender came running back with two officers. They were carrying flak jackets and helmets.

"Good job, Ender," Chad said. "You made it in only three minutes. All right, we have six and a half minutes left. First we get Mackenzie out of here."

They all looked a little confused.

"Ender, you get on Mackenzie's left side of the chair and, Bo, you on the right. I'm going to be watching underneath the chair at the pressure plate to make sure it doesn't move. You two are going to gradually put pressure on both sides of the chair while Kade gently holds Mackenzie's hands and slowly pulls her off of the chair. Then I will replace her on the chair."

"No!" Ender said.

"No?" Chad repeated, totally bewildered.

"I think I know where you're going with this. Lethal Weapon, am I right?"

Chad half-smiled.

"Oh no!" Kade said. "Not another movie."

"What?" Bo asked.

"Every time we get in some tight situation it reminds Chad of a movie." Kade looked at Chad. "Lethal Weapon 3, right, where Danny Glover is sitting on the toilet with a bomb underneath it?"

"Right you are, only it was Lethal Weapon 2."

Kade said, "Whatever. So this is your plan? I'm going to pull you off of the chair behind the desk before the bomb goes off. Oh, Chad, that is really thin."

———

Chad gave a flimsy smile.

"But I like it!" Kade said. "Let's do it."

"Except Ender said no."

All eyes went to Ender.

"Speed is the key," Ender said. "A pressure detonator will give a click and then go off. I'm thirty pounds lighter than Chad. I'll sit in the chair."

Everyone said nothing.

"Okay," Chad said. "No time for negotiations and voting. We go with Ender. Ender, you look under the chair and I'll be on Mac's left side."

They all got into position.

"Okay, gentlemen. We need to go slow but as fast as we can."

The gravity of the situation was intense but all worked together as Chad and Bo gradually pushed down on the chair and Kade tenderly pulled Mackenzie up.

When Mackenzie was up and clear, Ender got up from looking under the chair and carefully sat down while Kade looked under the chair at the pressure plate and Chad and Bo silently let up on the pressure. When Ender was securely in the seat, they all let out a breath.

"Okay, three minutes to go. Bo, you take Mackenzie out of the ..."

"No."

CHAPTER THIRTY-FIVE

CHAD LOOKED at Bo in exasperation.

"No, again? We don't have time for this."

Bo said, "You're right, we don't. You are the leader of this operation and are needed in case this goes south. Peter may be in custody but it's not over yet. You've got a family to protect."

"I agree," Kade said.

"Ditto," came from Ender.

Chad said, "There's no time for this."

"You're right, Chad," Kade said, "Scram! We'll be out in a minute."

Chad said nothing. Mackenzie grabbed his arm. "Come on, Chad. They'll be okay, I promise."

"You promise?"

Mackenzie looked over at Kade who nodded his head.

"Yes, I promise."

"Okay. We'll be right outside." They started for the door, Chad quickly turned around. "Did you get any cotton?"

Ender said, "Yes."

"Good, that's for your ears. Should be quite a blast."

Outside the warehouse Chad said, "I've never left my men for any reason. This isn't right."

"It's going to be okay."

Kade helped Ender put on the flak jacket and handed him a helmet. He and Bo then put on their jackets and helmets. They pulled the desk in front of where Ender was sitting and tipped it over so that the desktop was facing him.

"Okay," Kade said as he and Bo got behind the desk with the top between them and Ender. He took Ender by the right hand and wrist while Bo did the same with the left. "Obviously the real key to this is to jerk you as hard and fast as we can so that when the bomb goes off, at a minimum your head will be headed towards the floor and well behind the desk top. Any questions?"

"Yes," Ender said. "Who's buyin' tonight?"

"I am," Bo said, "Gladly."

Kade said. "Okay, on the count of three. One...two...three!"

The noise and concussion outside the warehouse was deafening and horrific. Chad's first thought was that nobody could possibly have lived through it. He felt sick as he bolted for the door. When he opened it smoke blasted him in the face. He couldn't even see down the hallway. He made his way along the wall and into the main area. It was still thick with smoke.

He hollered, "Kade, can you hear me? Bo, Ender, where are you?"

He heard nothing and still couldn't see. He began to panic. "Where are you guys?"

Finally the smoke started to empty through the hallway and a massive hole in the ceiling. As it cleared a little more he looked to where the chair had been. It was gone. That was understandable, but where was the desk?

He started looking around for his team as panic turned into terror, and then dread. "Please, God, no, no," he cried out. Then he heard it. A faint moan over in the corner, against the wall. He saw someone or something move. He sprinted over to a body that was lying face down. As he carefully rolled it over he realized it was Bo. Half of his face was covered in blood. His left arm was clearly broken.

"Bo, can you hear me?" Chad pleaded.

Bo was starting to come around slowly. He finally started to hear his name from what seemed very far away. He blinked a couple of times and Chad's face came into focus. He smiled and said, "Hey."

"Hold still, buddy. Help is on the way." He motioned for Mackenzie to come over and watch him.

Now in total panic, Chad looked around frantically. The smoke was clearing but not fast enough to see everywhere. Just as he was about to call out, he heard a slight giggle. He squinted in the direction of the sound, and through the thinning smoke saw Ender lying prone on Kade. Now they were starting to laugh uncontrollably. Chad sighed deeply with relief, and quickly walked over to them.

"Would you two like to be left alone?"

Kade looked at Chad, "I was just asking Ender if this means we're going steady." Ender carefully rolled off of Kade.

"Don't move too fast," Chad said. He could see blood on the floor. "Are either one of you hurting anywhere?"

Ender said, "More like are we *not* hurting anywhere? My ears are ringing and my body feels like it's been through a war."

———

"Your back is full of blood. Looks like you caught some shrapnel from the desk during the explosion. Lie still, help is on the way."

He looked at Kade. "I don't know what you're feeling but your ankle is definitely broken and there's a bone protruding from just above your elbow. You also have quite a bit of blood on top of your head. It looks like you didn't completely get all the way down behind the desk before the blast. The good news is I think I have the perfect roommate for you at the hospital; a detective from the United States recuperating from a gunshot wound."

Kade managed a smile even though the pain was starting to set in, "Sounds like a plan."

The ambulances arrived and Kade, Ender, and Bo were stabilized and ready for transport to the hospital. Bo seemed to be in the worst shape and was drifting in and out of consciousness. Mackenzie stood by Kade who was lying on a stretcher. She gently kissed him on his forehead. "How ya doin' my friend?"

"I've been better. Glad to be of service."

"Thanks for always being there, Kade. I wouldn't be here if it wasn't for you. Sydney is going to be proud of you, and I'm proud of you."

"Well now I'm feeling better already."

Chad walked over and Kade said, "I'm a little concerned about Strickland."

"Me, too. As we speak, the FBI and CIA are in negotiations with the local and national authorities to extradite Peter to the States. In fact we are going to transport him on the Hamilton Corporate Jet so no one outside of our little circle will know when and where he's going to be picked up and dropped off."

"Sounds good. The sooner the better." The attendants got ready to lift Kade into the ambulance. "Gotta go," Kade said. "Come and visit Sydney and me soon." It was obvious that he was in a lot of pain.

"See you in a few," Chad said. "You men are my heroes."

———

EIGHT HOURS later Kade lay in his hospital bed after a two-hour surgery to put his left arm and elbow back together. His right ankle had also been set and put in a cast. He was still a little groggy and had a morphine drip attached to his arm. He turned his head to the bed next to his.

"Hi, beautiful."

"Hi, yourself," Sydney said. "How are you feeling?"

"Well, since I'm gazing into the face of an angel, I must have died and gone to heaven."

"Ah, flattery will get you everywhere with me. Chad told me what you, Bo, and Ender did."

Kade said, "How are they? Have you heard anything yet?"

"Actually, better than you. No internal injuries for either of them. Bo has a broken arm and a concussion and, with the exception of a few cuts and bruises, Ender is okay. They were just here to see you, along with Chad and Mackenzie. They're in the cafeteria right now."

"So, when do you think we're getting out of here?"

"The doctor said most likely tomorrow. You have a concussion to go along with your arm and ankle injuries so they want to observe you for a day. I'm finished with my blood transfusions and will be free to go, too."

"How are you feeling, Syd?"

"To be honest, tired. The doctor said that's par for the course with a severe loss of blood." She smiled. "I'm going to need some real TLC."

"How about tonight after the lights go out?"

"Why, Michael Kincaid, you little devil. I may have to call a nurse for protection."

"Is she cute?" Kade asked.

"Let me put it this way, Michael, do you think a bop on the head with a metal bedpan would be good for your concussion?"

"Ooh, message received loud and clear!"

"Is this guy giving you trouble already?" Chad asked as he, Mackenzie, Ender and Bo walked in. Bo was on crutches.

"Nothing that I can't handle," Sydney giggled.

"I'm sure of that," Chad said.

"How are you feeling?" Bo asked.

Kade looked at Bo with his head bandaged and his cast and crutches. "Probably about the same as you. Do you still have the ringing in your ears?"

"What?" Ender said.

Kade smiled. "Exactly." He nodded at Chad. "I gotta give it to you, your plan saved us all. And look at you. As usual, not a scratch on you."

Chad got a little defensive. "I didn't want to leave, but you..."

Kade laughed out loud and then groaned, "I'm just kidding, Chad. We were all where we were supposed to be. No one died on our side and we finally got Peter Strickland, right?"

Chad frowned as he looked down. "We lost him again."

CHAPTER THIRTY-SIX

KADE JERKED up as best he could. "What!? Please don't tell me..."

Chad interrupted, "It was an inside job. One of the arresting officers was in cahoots with a guard at the jail. Peter disappeared without any incident."

Kade slumped back in the bed. "All that work for nothing. That guy is a ghost. We are never going to catch him and bring him in alive." He was silent for a second. "I'm sorry, Chad. No more promises. If I get within a mile of that guy, he dies and that will be the end of it. I can't believe we're back to square one."

"Not exactly," Ender said.

"What do you mean, not exactly?"

Chad said, "We've always had something that Strickland has never had."

"What's that?"

"Neal."

"Has that boy come up with some good stuff on Strickland?"

"That he has. First let me tell you what we know for sure. After the officer and guard were persuaded to confess what they knew, we learned that Peter has a private airstrip less than three miles from the casino and only five from his villa. He was taken directly to the airstrip where he boarded his private jet to somewhere in the Middle East."

Kade said, "The Middle East is a pretty big area."

"Yes, it is," Chad said. "But that's when Neal took over. There are five well-known havens for those who don't want to be found. One of them is in the Middle East, or to be exact, The United Arab Emirates."

"The envelope please," Kade said.

Chad smiled, "The city of Dubai. Dubai is the Las Vegas of the Persian Gulf. It also has private islands available for purchase by those with funds."

"So you think he may be in Dubai, huh? Is that all?"

"Oh no, my friend. Neal was just getting started. He already has records of Peter's finances and locations all over the world that he uses."

"Any in Dubai?"

"Bingo. Not only have some funds gone through the Bank of Dubai, but over twenty million has stayed there."

Kade asked, "Any unusual purchases from that account?"

Bo said, "Right you are again. One of those purchases was for a private island for seven million and construction has been going on for the last five months."

"Sounds encouraging but how do you know it's his little island?"

Chad said, "I'm pretty close to certain."

"How close, let's say on a scale of one to ten?"

"About a nine and a half."

"That's reasonably certain. What aren't you telling me?"

"Well, if you'd quit interrupting, I'll tell you," Chad teased.

Kade smiled.

"The name on the account is Piero Salvestro."

Kade still said nothing.

"Paul Stevens aka Peter Strickland. Peter is consistent if nothing else. Remember that's how we were able to crack the code on his account with the two hundred seventy-five million in it. First name starts with a P and last name with an S. Piero Salvestro."

"Okay, it's a little weak, but I'll bite. What else?"

"Two things," Chad said. "First, we have a satellite hookup that is going to show us anyone who is on the property. There has been some activity in the last four hours."

"Peter?"

"No, not yet, but we should see him soon if he's coming."

"You said two things."

Chad said, "My gut tells me this is Peter. The satellite will confirm it."

"Why didn't you say that in the first place? I'll go with your instincts over the facts any day!" He paused. "No way you're doing this without me."

Chad looked at Kade's bandaged head, his heavily wrapped elbow and his elevated leg with the cast on it. "Don't worry; I won't do this without you, pal." He turned to Ender and Bo. "Or you two. We'll verify through the satellite that it is Peter and then give you guys a few days to do some healing. Okay?"

All three nodded.

"There's one more thing," Chad said. "When we get to Peter in Dubai, we are *not* going to kill him."

Kade sat up again in his bed. "You've got to be kidding me. That man has to die! There is no extradition from Dubai. Come on, Chad; are you crazy? He wants to destroy you and almost *has* twice now."

Chad said, "I didn't say he didn't have to die. I just said we weren't going to do it."

CHAPTER THIRTY-SEVEN

KADE LOOKED over at Bo and Ender. They both shrugged their shoulders. He looked back at Chad.

"Don't worry, boys. I have a plan. If it works, Peter will be done permanently."

"And if it doesn't?" Kade asked.

"Then we'll go with your proposal."

———

"WHAT DO you think of Chad's idea, Syd?" Kade and Sydney were alone in Kade's room. Chad, Mackenzie, Ender, and Bo had gone to dinner.

"It certainly is ingenious, and I think it's got teeth."

"So you think it will work?"

"I do."

"Me, too."

———

Two weeks later...

THE PHONE RANG twice before he picked it up. "Hello?"

"I'd like to speak to Peter please."

"You must have the wrong number, mister. There's nobody here by that name."

"Oh, I beg to differ. You just be a good boy and tell him that his old friend Chad Hamilton is on the phone. He'll take my call."

"I'm telling you there's nobody by that name that lives here." He started to hang up.

"Okay," Chad said. "I'll just warn you that when you tell Peter that I asked for him and you didn't take the call, you're a dead man."

He said nothing.

"I'll wait while you're contemplating the last moments of your life."

There was silence for about sixty seconds.

"Chad, what a pleasant surprise! You are the most amazing man I have ever met. I've never known someone who seems to have more lives than a cat. I won't ask you how you found me. The fact that you did is astonishing. Maybe we could discuss it at some future date over dinner."

"Actually, Peter, that's why I'm calling. How about dinner tomorrow night here in Dubai?"

Strickland said nothing.

"Cat got your tongue, Peter? How about the Al Sarab Rooftop Lounge? I understand the cuisine is excellent. You bring one of your boys and I'll bring Kade."

"Sounds delicious. Are we going to have a shoot out at the OK Corral?"

"That would be fun, Peter, but no. I'm tired of all this. I want my life back and my family protected. I plan on making you an offer that I hope you won't want to refuse. Let's end this."

"Even though I don't completely believe you, you've really got my curiosity piqued." There was a short pause. "Okay, Chad, you're on."

"Good. We'll meet outside so you can check us for weapons and we'll do the same. But as you know, the penalty for foreigners is severe in Dubai for any funny stuff."

"That I do, Chad. Need I remind you that there are no extradition laws here?"

"I'm well aware of that, Peter. That's why I'm trying to end this. You don't want to spend the rest of your life on the run, do you?"

"Point taken, Chad. See you tomorrow night." He hung up the phone.

"You don't believe him, do you?" Strickland's bodyguard asked.

"Not for a minute, Brady. But I know for a fact that Hamilton's family is everything to him, the poor sap. It may cause him to make a tiny little mistake and that's all I'll need."

"What makes you so sure?"

"Because I'm better than him."

———

At four o'clock the next day Chad, Kade, Ender, and Bo met in Chad's hotel room. "All right, I think we're ready," He said to Ender and Bo who were both dressed in black. "There shouldn't be much security at the villa. From what we can tell from the satellite photos, you may only have a little resistance getting in. I think Strickland feels safe here in Dubai with no extradition laws. He may beef it up in a day or two now that he knows I know he is here, but by then we will have executed our plan. Have you guys got the package ready?"

Bo said, "All set. This should be a piece of cake. Just make sure you have a nice long dinner with Peter and when he leaves he's not suspicious at all."

Kade said, "It will be our finest hour."

"As long as you don't lose your temper," Chad said. "What happens if he says something nasty about Sydney?"

"Not a problem. I'll just smile and lean over and choke him to death."

"Okay, boys. We'll meet back here later tonight and see if the plan is working or it's back to the drawing board."

Kade said, "There is no drawing board. If this fails we go to plan K, and that's me. End of discussion."

CHAD AND KADE arrived at the restaurant at seven-fifty. As they were getting out of their rental car, Peter Strickland and his bodyguard drove into the parking lot in his grey Mercedes. They walked over to the car as Strickland was exiting.

"Chad, so good to see you. And Kade, it looks like you're healing well. I hope you're not still angry with me?"

Kade stayed silent.

"Okay, Peter, let's cut the niceties and get on with it."

Peter's bodyguard, Brady, frisked both Chad and Kade, and Kade did the same to them. Then they walked into the hotel and took the elevator to the top floor where the restaurant was located. Chad had made reservations the day before, so they were shown to their table without delay.

After a little small talk with their server, Strickland started the conversation.

"Chad, I must admit I was in total shock when you called yesterday. I figured you would eventually find me, but not this quick. To be perfectly honest with you," he paused. "We are going to be honest with each other, aren't we?"

Chad said nothing, but then he changed his mind.

"Look, Peter. If we're going to be honest, I don't like you and you don't like me."

"True, and I am getting tired of this. I'm good at what I do and I could do this for a long time, but I would like to end it. So you said you had some kind of resolution for me? I sincerely doubt it, but I'm all ears."

Chad said, "First of all, Peter, there's something about Kade and me that you don't know."

"What would that be?"

"We are under special assignment with the FBI."

Strickland laughed. "Right, and I am actually a priest in disguise."

"Nevertheless I report straight to the Director, and ever since we arrived in Seoul, Korea, we have also had the cooperation of the CIA. I had the authority to call in a hit squad over a week ago when we located your villa and to terminate you."

Peter lost most of his arrogance. "Then why didn't you order it?" he challenged.

"Lord knows I should have. In the last eight months many innocent people have died, most of them your own people. Your stooge Duke kidnapped my sister and I was shot and left for dead. Only by no small miracle am I still here. Then more men stormed my house at a barbeque, putting my parents and friends in jeopardy. Do I need to go on?"

"Cut to the chase, Chad. What are you proposing?"

"I don't have the authority to pardon you and allow you to come back to the States; no one does. You burned those bridges when those two agents died at the courthouse when you escaped last year. But I can do a couple of things for you."

Strickland had a blank look on his face and said nothing.

"First, you can go back to Rio and live your life there and no one from the U.S. will bother you. I know you have some insiders within law enforcement there so it should be business as usual."

Strickland stayed silent.

"Two, I'll give you two hundred and fifty million to go back to Rio and forget you ever knew me. Promise me this and that you'll stay away from my family and the money is yours."

Strickland stared at Chad momentarily and then looked at Kade, who sat there looking straight into Peter's eyes, showing no emotion.

"After all we've been through and knowing that I am determined to destroy you, how can you even begin to trust me at my word?"

Chad said, "Let's get one thing straight, Peter, I will never trust you. If you accept my offer, I will know where you are at all times. I have the resources to do that and you know it. If I even think or feel that you are near my family, I'll unleash your worst nightmare."

"And what is that?"

CHAPTER THIRTY-EIGHT

CHAD SMILED. "Did you know that Kade was in the CIA?"

Strickland's eyes moved towards Kade, who for the first time smiled.

"Kade was an assassin and one of the best snipers in the world. You remember when he shot Duke from the trees three hundred yards away? That was about a quarter of his capabilities. He had over fifty kills while with the company. After a few years he got tired of it, but he can still make the shot. I've been to the range with him at least once a month. After what you did to his lady friend, Sydney, he's begging to finish the job."

Strickland sat still and finally took a deep breath. "Well, Chad, you certainly seem to be holding all the cards. Do I get to think about this or do you require an immediate answer?"

"You have eighteen hours, Peter. I'll call you at three tomorrow afternoon."

"Three o'clock, huh? Okay, Chad, you've got me. I'll seriously think about it."

"Oh, Peter, you don't sound like you're taking this seriously. Did I mention that the hit squad is ready and can deploy in hours? And one more thing; that beautiful helicopter that you have sitting on the pad at your villa? I think you'll find that it has a headache. Won't be much use until you can get a new engine for it."

You could have cut the silence with a knife.

Chad and Kade got up. "Three o'clock then."

As they began to walk out, Kade leaned over to get close to Peter's face. "Please say *no* tomorrow."

———

"EVERYTHING GO OKAY AT THE VILLA?" Kade asked.

Ender said, "Perfect. Went off without a hitch. The helicopter is disabled and the package delivered."

"Great job, guys," Chad said. "I know it's late but I ordered room service. Nachos, enchiladas, and a boatload of tamales."

"In Dubai?" Bo said. "How in the world did you...never mind. I forgot, you're Chad Hamilton."

"Don't you forget it," Kade said. "And I'm going to make us some great margaritas."

"I have no doubt," Ender smiled.

"So, Mr. Hamilton," Bo said, "do you think Strickland will accept your offer?"

"Not a chance. The whole ploy was to get Peter away from his pad. Is everything in place, Bo?"

"All set, Chad. I do have one major question."

"Ask away."

"Did you order guacamole with that food?"

———

AT TWO FORTY-FIVE the next afternoon, Chad and Kade were sitting in chairs at the water's edge. They could see Strickland's little island from there. Chad had powerful binoculars hanging around his neck.

Kade reached for a walkie-talkie type device. "Is everything ready and in place?"

"All set," Ender answered.

Kade looked at Chad who nodded.

"Okay, make the call," he told Ender.

Chad went into his pocket and pulled out a cell phone he had purchased the day before, and punched in the number.

"Chad, right on time. You continue to impress me."

"Hello, Peter. I trust you had a good night after we left?"

"Yes, but I must admit you put a bit of a damper on it. I'll tell you, Chad, I don't like being issued ultimatums. You certainly seemed to have put me in an awkward position."

"I assure you, Peter, it was purely intentional."

"Ah, a sense of humor to the end. I like that." Peter paused a moment for effect. "Your offer was very tempting. Getting my casino back, and my life in Rio as it was, and then two hundred and fifty million dollars. Wow."

"So?"

"So here's the thing, Chad, I have a pretty good life here and can stay as long as I need to. The money was tempting but in case you haven't noticed, I'm very good at making money."

"So your answer is no?"

"Did you actually think you could threaten me, Chad? Or that sabotaging my helicopter would stop me from escaping? Can you give me back my life in Boston or Miami? No. I will not rest until I've taken everything from you: your money, your family, and then your life."

While Peter was speaking, Chad saw a small boat approaching the island through his binoculars.

"Is that your final answer, Peter?"

"My whole life will be spent ruining you, Chad Hamilton. As long as I have any breath in me I'll make your life a living hell."

The doorbell rang.

"Sounds like you have company, Peter. I'll hold."

Strickland stared at his phone and then made his way to the door as his man Brady opened it. About twelve uniformed men stood there dressed in olive green uniforms with dark green berets.

"Mr. Salvestro?"

Peter said, "I'm Piero Salvestro."

The man in charge actually gave Peter a nod. "I'm Captain Adham Barum of the Dubai police."

"What's this all about, Captain?"

"We've received a rather disturbing report that there are drugs on these premises and that you, Mr. Salvestro, are responsible for them. A very serious accusation, sir."

"A false accusation, Captain."

"Are you aware, sir, of the penalty in Dubai for drug trafficking?"

"I know that the penalty for drug trafficking anywhere in the world is serious, Captain, usually ending up with prison time and a huge fine."

"Not in Dubai, sir. Neither of those is used here. No sir, the penalty for such a crime here is death by firing squad."

Strickland felt sick to his stomach. "Be that as it may, Captain, there are no drugs here."

Captain Barum held up a piece of paper. "We need to search your home, sir. Please be seated."

"By all means, Captain. You'll find nothing here. I don't deal in drugs."

Captain Barum nodded to his men who scattered and began their search. Two of them stayed with their Captain who was standing near Strickland and Brady.

Strickland realized he still had the phone in his hands. Then reality set in as his stomach did a complete flop.

"Are you still on the line, Chad?"

"Oh, I wouldn't miss your party for the world, Peter. Is it a costume party? Seems like everyone's dressed like cops."

As Chad was speaking, two of the police officers walked into the living room. One of them threw down a big plastic bag on the coffee table that looked like a bunch of white powder. The other one set down another plastic bag containing packages of strapped one hundred dollar bills.

"Well well," said Captain Barum. "What do we have here?"

"We found this in the closet in the guest room. There's a lot more of these drugs and money."

"That's ridiculous," Strickland screamed. "It's obvious that I've been set up. Who told you these were here?"

"Actually, Mr. Salvestro, we received a call from your government."

"Whose government? I have *no* government."

"From an agency of the United States. We know about your dealings in Boston, Miami, and Rio de Janeiro. You managed to escape twice, Mr. Strickland."

Peter said, "They have no jurisdiction here. Dubai has no extradition laws."

"Oh, they are quite aware of that. But they did give us enough evidence and probable cause to check you and your residence out, and look what we found. No need for extradition. We will handle it right here in Dubai."

"I've been set up!" He put the phone to his ear. "You did this, didn't you, Hamilton?"

"Good bye, Peter." The phone clicked off.

EPILOGUE

ONE MONTH LATER...

"Oooh. That smells out of this world, Chad."

"Thanks, Dad," Chad said. "I keep telling everyone that my barbecue chicken is the best."

Kade said, "Well, lets just hope this barbecue at the Hamilton home doesn't end up like the last one eight months ago."

"Don't even mention that dreadful day!" Chad's mother said. "All those bad men and guns."

"I, for one, thought it was very exciting," Chad's grandpa said.

"You would," his new bride Alice said. "You Hamiltons are all alike, too much action."

"Guilty as charged, Alice," Chad said. "I'm so sorry about that, Mother. It will never happen again, I promise."

Chad glanced over at Kade and gave him a stare that said *I hope.* Bo noticed the look on Chad's face.

"You needn't worry about Peter Strickland anymore, Chad, he's dead."

"I know he's as good as dead, Bo, but I still worry that he could be pulling some strings from his prison cell. He's done it before."

Bo said, "I know, Chad, but that's what I'm telling you, Peter Strickland is literally dead."

"What?"

"He was found hanging in his cell. Did it with his own belt."

Chad shook his head, "I, I can't believe it. Peter Strickland wouldn't give up so easily."

"Evidently he did, Chad," Kade said. "Maybe he preferred it to a firing squad."

Kade's and Bo's eyes met but they said nothing.

Then Kade turned back to Chad. "Case closed, my good man. It's over."

Chad stared at Kade and Bo for a long time, the wheels turning in his head, and finally took a deep breath and then a smile lit up his face. "All right then. Let's eat," he said.

Mackenzie walked up and slipped her arm through Chad's. "Everything okay? You all looked so serious for a minute."

Chad looked at Kade, Bo, and Ender. "Couldn't be better, Mac."

"You can say that again." Chad's good friend and baseball partner, Treat, said as he strolled up to the group.

Chad said, "You got some good news for me, bro?"

Treat grinned from ear to ear.

"You got him?!" Chad shouted.

"That we did, my friend!"

"Did what?" Mackenzie asked.

Chad could hardly contain himself. "We got Skeeter Lefleur!"

"What is a Skeeter La Who?" Sydney asked.

"He's our new manager. Montreal now has a leader. And, the city just voted and has overwhelmingly picked the Expos as their name. Evidently they feel like there's some unfinished business from before, and I agree. Skeeter is French Canadian, played minor league baseball in Montreal in the sixties, was a great major league manager, and now at age seventy-two, has agreed to be our manager. He will be perfect for those first couple of seasons while we are trying to develop our young talent."

"And then what?" Chad's mother asked. "It's just a silly old game!"

"It may be just a silly old game to you, Mother, but Treat and I are fulfilling our childhood dream. And then what, you ask? How about the World Series?"

———

So, can you hear it, Doug?

That's my sigh of relief. I can hardly believe it and it's even harder to say out loud... IT'S OVER! We finally caught up with Peter Strickland in Rio but he got away temporarily. Our final confrontation in Dubai ended in his capture and incarceration for the possession and sale of drugs, an offense punishable by death from a firing squad. I wonder where he got the drugs? Hmmmm. The only thing is that it will never go to trial. Three weeks after his arrest he apparently hanged himself in his cell. I say apparently because I don't believe it. I firmly believe that with their CIA connections, Kade and Bo got to Peter somehow to protect me. With him alive I never would've been able to totally relax and my family's safety would always be in jeopardy. I don't think I could've ever done it, but deep, I mean way down deep where we don't like to go very often, I'm glad. Time to move forward.

On a higher note Ellie is doing great. Her new family is in the process of adopting her. She's going to need therapy for a long time but everyone is optimistic and I'm pleased with her progress. By the way, thanks to Aunt Mackenzie, I'm Uncle Chad. How about that, Doug? I'm going to have to make an honest woman out of her. Did I tell you that in a weak moment I asked her to marry me? Who would've thought that this old confirmed bachelor could fall head over heels in love so fast? I'm so looking forward to spending the rest of my life with her.

Well, Doug, gotta go. We just got Skeeter Lefleur as our manager. Right now I'm in negotiations with the Red Sox to get their golden boy, Ty Roundy. He was my superstar with the Springfield Rebels. We need him and I want him. Don't bet against me, Doug. Life is good!

THANK YOU

Thanks for reading Revenge, the second Chad Hamilton novel. The next book in the series is Kade. As an independent author, what drives the success of this book, and others to follow, are reviews. If you enjoyed reading about Chad and friends, then please post a review on Amazon so others can find the series as well. And don't forget to tell your friends about the series!

You can visit my website at www.mikeshaneauthor.com for more info on the Chad Hamilton Series and to join the mailing list to keep up with future releases and promotions.

You can "like" my page on Facebook at www.facebook.com/Mike-ShaneAuthor to stay up to date on my newest writing adventures and get a behind the scenes look before books are published.

I love to hear from readers so feel free to email me at Mike@mike-shaneauthor.com.

AUTHOR'S NOTE

As always, a special thanks to my wife and best friend Linda who's been by my side all the way. I couldn't continue writing without her strength and support. I'd also like to thank my friends and family who have encouraged me to press on after the first Chad Hamilton book. A big thank you to my readers. I will continue working on the series as long as you all keep reading. I'm currently working on the next adventure!

BOOKS BY MIKE SHANE:

Good Intentions – Chad Hamilton Series book 1

Revenge – Chad Hamilton Series book 2

Kade - Chad Hamilton Series book 3 Coming in the Fall of 2019